BUSINE'

BlaqRayn ...

The Boss Lady's

Urban Fiction

ᑒ ᐁ

𝓑usiness 𝓛eft

UNFINISHED

ᑒ ᐁ

𝒯he 𝓑oss 𝓛ady

BUSINESS LEFT UNFINISHED

BlaqRayn Publishing

134 Andrew Drive

Reidsville NC, 27320.

Printed in the United States of America

ISBN: 9781790316755

Printed by KDP 2018

Published by BlaqRayn Publishing Plus 2018

Dedication

This book is dedicated to

Aaron J. Brewer,

Alexandrea J. Johnson,

Domynique Shelby and

Rosa L. Prazak -

My Why's.

Foreword

A story of love, loss, redemption and a smidgen of something else…WHAT???

Here is a not so classic tale of love. We have a story of seven people and how their lives play out in ways unimaginable. Forbidden love, loves tragic loss, loving again and the stuff that horror movies are made of...all in one neat little package. We will begin with Mya and her relationship.

Some may call it the seven-year itch, which would have been appropriate, if in fact they had been together for seven years. Mya knew going into this relationship that it may not work out, there were tale - tale signs of things going bad sooner or later. Let's go back to the beginning of the end , when everything seemed to change.

"Unfinished business will always come for you. Whatever you fail to kill will hunt your children, or, the next generation."

Samuel T. Padmore

Chapter 1

I Go To Work

This story begins on a cold winter morning, the kind of day for hot chocolate and flannel pajamas. As Mya was coming out of her deep slumber, she dreaded the thought...another day.

Mya Parker was 30 years old and not exactly sure if things would ever be the way she thought her life should be. Her skin is that of rich and smooth mocha fudge, with a pair of eyes that always seemed to be smiling. Her nose was small but sharp and it looked good on her. Her lips were thin but again, they were fitting to her face.

Mya had been through a lot in her young life; some good and some awful. Mya, a hopeless romantic, was not happy with her life. Compared to the few friends she had, her life was the epitome of happiness and contentment. Mya could not, nor would not admit to her friends that she was miserable. She was the only guide they had to what happiness resembled. She didn't like that.

The man in her life was the best thing she had going for her in the longest of times. His name was Eric McGhee. Eric was ten years Mya's senior and he was fine. He had the most beautiful smile Mya had ever seen. His eyes were light brown and just the right almond shape. His nose was broad and his bridge was full. His hair was short and wavy; skin smooth, like chocolate milk. Her prince charming is what she called him. Eric and Mya had been together for some time and gave all appearances of being happy. No one would have thought otherwise.

It was winter, a time for hibernating, like the bears. Typical of winter, it was snowing, a blizzard if you will. Mya was no stranger to cold weather but that didn't mean she liked it any more than anyone else. She woke with the clock radio playing a sultry tune by one of her favorite female artists **Anita Baker**. Mya was not a morning person but she knew it was time to get up. Organization was a skill Mya had perfected to her own degree as far as getting herself together. Her simplest trick, get it done the night before.

Usually once out of the bed, everything else is easy. She decided to grab some fruit and some graham crackers for her morning breakfast. Good, just enough time to put on her coat and head for the bus. Mya noticed it had snowed much more than she realized and wished she had put on her long boots. Whew!

She made it just in time, here comes the bus. Noticing this morning's bus was more crowded than usual, she became angry. As she made her way back to her self-appointed seat, Mya noticed there is someone already sitting there. *Although he may be cute, he **is** in my seat*, Mya declares to herself. *Oh well, I guess I will just sit next to him and see what, if anything, he's all about.*

Chapter 2

The Wheels On The Bus

How he hated riding the bus. Not that he was all that, but, in his small mind, he believed it. *Here comes all these damned people and I don't want any of them sitting next to me,* he thought to his narcissist self. Hamilton Oliver III, *Oli*, to his friends, was your first class jerk. An asshole was the word most used to describe him and he was okay with that.

Oli was the kind of man you either loved or hated, there was no happy medium with him. Most people that had any contact with him, choose the latter. His mother loved him but she was biased. Oli was tall and attractive and he knew it, thus his downfall. He was conceited as hell and let everyone know it, whether they cared or not.

THE BOSS LADY

Although he was an arrogant ass, he was just in his claims. Oli had heavy, dark features that a lot of women found very attractive. His hair was thick with enough texture to create an ocean of beautiful black waves. The color of his skin reminded one of Georgia clay; it was gorgeous, with red undertones. Eyes are the windows to the soul from what I have heard and, based on his eyes, Oli had a deep dark soul. His eyes were mysterious and alluring, creating a sense of adventure, leading to misadventure once you got to know him. His mouth was a dentist dream, the most perfect set of teeth you have ever seen. All in all, he was the complete package, at least appearance wise that is.

Their eyes met, but so what. Mya thought to herself, *okay buddy, it's time to share my seat.* Oli saw her coming and being the jerk that he is, he placed his briefcase on the seat just as she is about to sit down.

"Damn it! Excuse me!" Mya said through clenched teeth. "I was going to sit there."

BUSINESS LEFT UNFINISHED

Oli peered around the bus and points to a seat somewhere other than where he was and suggested that she sit there.

"You've got some nerve," Mya says, now a little hot under the collar. "You are not going to dictate to me where I will sit Mr. Man. You are not even a regular rider on this bus, so by right, I should be telling you where the hell to sit!" Mya was one spitfire of a woman once you pissed her off; there was no shutting her up until she finished..

She had just about had enough of him when he apologized, removed his briefcase from the seat and even offered her the window seat. *That's more like it* Mya thought as she accepted both his seat and apology. Everyone on the bus looked on and shook their heads ; it was too early in the morning to be fussing over a seat. Sit down and shut the hell up!

This is not a good way to start a Monday morning, they both thought, daring not to say a word to one another. Today's bus ride lasted about one hour and Mya planned to get in a quick nod, or at least that's what she thought.

The dream was sexy, even for seven in the morning. It was a heart starter for sure. Just when the best part was about to happen, Eric turned into Oli and scared Mya half to death. She woke with such a start, she almost knocked Oli on the floor. If looks could kill, Hamilton Oliver III would have been dead on arrival at the next stop.

Chapter 3

A Day In MY Life

Finally they were downtown. Mya was an editor for one of Ohio's leading publishing corporations, **The L.D. Corp** and she loved her job. As she glanced up and saw her building looming over all the other skyscrapers, she was proud to work there. She started gathering her belongings as Mya's stop was the last one on the route.

Oli chanced handing Mya one of his business cards as he flashed her winning smile. Unbeknownst to Mya, she had been chosen. The look on Oli's face as he presented the card, made her warm and fuzzy. Her curiosity was piqued. His card was a thing of sheer elegance. It was blue, with shiny gold facing. The detailing was amazing as the letters were in a hieroglyphic style and like their possessor, stunning. It read, **_Hamilton Oliver III, Attorney-at-Law._**

"An arrogant lawyer…humph. Don't we have enough of them already in the world?" she mumbled to herself, presumably under her breath. As she took the card, she gave him a wan smile and prepared to finally get of this damned bus.

It appeared, as she entered her office, that not a lot of people had shown up for work today. Mya thought she would be livid, after all the effort exerted to get here but then she thought she would definitely be grateful for the peace.

As she suspected, less than half the staff had shown up for work but it was just like Mya to be different and come in on the day of a blizzard, with another expected sometime throughout the day.

"Way to go Mighty Mya," she chided with herself. There were many options and opportunities on how to make this day work as a career building day. This was going to be a wonderful day!

Mya chuckled as she prepared to set into motion the Mya Parker work site. None of the executives or their assistants were in, which meant she could use the "Big Editing Room". Mya had almost fainted the first time they shown her the "big room" as it was called. It was the biggest room she'd ever lain her eyes on. Everything a writer, editor, or publisher would ever need to do could be done right here in this room. If it was not here, it was not made yet. She finally figured out, if she was smart, she could go to the room and make magic happen. Today could be the day her life began to change in many ways.

Mya was as close to being in heaven at this moment as she would ever be. She goes in and turns "it" on, the big red button that controls all the power in the room. As the computers and printers start to load, the coffee maker starts to drip.

THE BOSS LADY

"Now, that is what I call efficient," Mya voiced out loud. Being the only person in your work area can have major fringe benefits. She was going to do her life's work today, until it was ready to go out.

Mya had her own story to tell; her autobiography. It started as a book report for her high school English class. She'd continued to work on it even through college. It had flourished, had grown and now was her golden opportunity to shine as never before. Not only as an editor, but also as a writer.

In the big room alone, Mya could use the edit machine for her own work while she inched over her assigned work. As she watched her dream transform from just words and thoughts to a real manuscript, she lost track of time and space.

The day was breezing by and had it not been for the phone in her office ringing, she would not have even noticed it was well past 3:30 p.m. She dashed to her office, arriving in time to hear Eric's voice on her machine requesting she pick up if she were there. *I am here* she thought, *but I will not let you know it* as she finished listening to his message. *So he wants to get together tonight, now why am I not surprised? It has only been a week or so since I have even seen him in person so of course it is time for us to "get together".*

Mya had made a promise to herself that no matter how bad she wanted to be with Eric, she wasn't going to give in to him every time he found it convenient. She couldn't continue to give her goodies away without receiving anything more permanent and worthwhile in return. She was more than just some man's sexual object.

"I deserve better and more, dammit!!!" This came out in a violent whisper as her anger began to rise.

Eric was a determined young man, a hard worker and a man with a goal. He was relentless in that no matter what the cost, he was going to reach his goals. He loved Mya. He had never loved a woman like he loved her.

Eric remembered when he'd first seen Mya. He'd been downtown and found himself staring at her as he was heading for a meeting with one of his colleagues. He'd been on the elevator when she got on and was awestruck by her beauty. Mya also found herself staring at Eric's strikingly strong features. They only acknowledged one another with a brief nod, then Mya got off the elevator.

Over the next four or five months, there were other "occasions" that brought Eric to the *A.J. Johnson Building*. He made it a mission on each occasion to "run" into Mya, just to say hello.

One day, he got up enough nerve to ask her out. She was actually pretty shy and was reluctant at first but she listened to her heart and accepted.

BUSINESS LEFT UNFINISHED

To be quite honest, they have not had an easy go of it. During various stages of their relationship, faithfulness was an ongoing issue. Eric tried to ease her pain with apologies and gifts, being on his best behavior and because she believed she loved him, she continued to forgive. Despite the red flags, she plunged forward, leery yet determined to make it work. He'd said he loved her more than he would ever be able to show or tell her.

Eric wanted to believe what he was telling Mya (he was pretty sure he didn't love her) and he was less sure he could be faithful to any one woman. He would shudder at the thought of having access to only one for the rest of his life. He wasn't sure he was that guy but he was ***damn*** sure he didn't want Mya know that. Love or no love, faithfulness or not, he wasn't quite ready to let her go.

So, she fought the urge to pick up the phone, call Eric and set up a time to see him. *I must finish my work* she reminded herself sternly. *I cannot afford distractions by Eric or anyone else!*

THE BOSS LADY

It was then that Mya realized she was starving; she hadn't eaten all day. She had been so consumed by her work, but now seemed like a great time to rest her mind and feed her brain. The weather had gone from blizzard conditions to just a few flurries, so she decided to brave the elements and go across the street for a nice hot meal.

Oli had been in court all morning. The case he was handling was the biggest of his career and he needed to win. He was going over notes as he tried to eat a sandwich. Before he looked up, he felt her presence. *The girl of my dreams* he thought as he caught her eye and smiled.

Oh my God! Twice in one day. How cursed can one person's luck be, Mya ranted inwardly as she noticed Oli smiling in her direction. *I just know he's not smiling at me. Why would he be smiling at me? I don't even like him, I DO NOT!* Too bad she was having a hard time convincing herself of that fact.

BUSINESS LEFT UNFINISHED

Oli, however, was in love and had no doubt in **his** mind whatsoever. She was the woman from the bus, the woman of his dreams. Oli rarely even glanced at a woman, because once spending a few moments in his presence, no woman gave him the time of day. Oli was a bit of a misunderstood kinda guy. As arrogant and conceited as he appeared to be, he had a softer side he shielded from most people. A defense mechanism some would say. As soon as he'd seen her, in rare form, on the bus, he'd known he had to have her. When Mya stood up to him in that most condescending of ways, he'd known...somehow, someway she was going to love him. He was going to make her his to love forever.

Unfortunately for Oli, Mya decided she would take her lunch back to her office and eat in peace, while still working on her masterpiece. She paid for her food and began to leave. When she looked up, her path was blocked by the one person she did not want anything to do with. Oli, the arrogant lawyer from the bus this morning with that most beautifully done business card.

"Can I help you," she asked, not really meaning it to sound so nice.

"Well yes, as a matter of fact you can," Oli answered in spite of himself. "I would like to apologize for my behavior this morning by taking you to dinner, at your convenience of course." Mya felt as though her bottom lip had hit the floor…

Meanwhile, in his office across town, Eric was at odds with himself. He had not talked to Mya, yet he felt as though something was wrong. Whatever it was, he just couldn't put his finger on it but he was going to find out.

I know Mya loves me he assured himself, *even though I haven't been completely upfront with her. We haven't seen each other in quite some time, but I know she trusts me and I trust her and that everything is okay.*

"Alright, there I have said it but do I believe it? I had better say yes to keep from going off the deep end but, somehow, I don't feel it like I used to…but why? Maybe she knows about my other activities and has some of her own...could that be it?" He had to make sure that none of their paths crossed because the fallout from that blow up would be catastrophic. He'd better get it together soon. It wasn't a good idea for him to be seen around the office in a daze and talking to himself.

Chapter 4

So, What Do You Think About That?

Autumn Matthews was peeking out of her Glenview Avenue window at the snow. How she longed for the snow, it was her favorite seasonal thing. Paired with the nice, strong arms of a man around her, holding her tight.

The man she wanted and needed, at least in her mind, was one off limits to her. Autumn was the owner of a small yet lucrative consignment shop called *I Got Just What You Need*. It was a quaint little shop in a great general location. She was happy with it at first but now she was bored. She needed something new to pique her interest. She grew restless easily and was always in pursuit of the newest thing to bring her excitement and fulfillment.

Autumn was a pretty woman in her mid-twenties who knew what she wanted. She was a bit of a brat so she was never pleased when she didn't get her way. She had the beauty of a model. Her skin was caramel smooth, her hair was shoulder length and gorgeous. With long legs and a perfect hourglass shape, she was a vision of beauty and the envy of many.

As she smiled at a passing snowflake, she wondered how she could make Eric McGhee hers and hers alone. She was accustomed to getting her way and this wouldn't turn out any differently.

Chapter 5

Thank You For Being A Friend

Mya could not believe the type of day she was having. First a blizzard, then the call from Eric and now this. Yet, through it all, it wasn't as atrocious as some other days. Still shocked and intrigued over Oli's invitation to dinner, she needed to call her best friend and get her opinion on just how to handle this delicate situation. This was something she couldn't have foreseen coming in a million years.

Angel Greenlee was busy with the kids. While she did not have any of her own, she enjoyed running the daycare center she was part owner of with her sister. Angel was a lonely person with a lot of love to give but no one to receive it. Men were truly blind if they couldn't see the treasure in her.

BUSINESS LEFT UNFINISHED

Angel stood about five foot eight and on the thick side but sis wore it well. Her complexion was deep dark and she didn't believe she was beautiful because of it. She'd bought into that whole lie about darker skin tones. She possessed big brown eyes with those long lashes to die for. Her skin was as smooth as silky dark chocolate.

Due to the darkness of her skin and those awesome eyes, she was quite alluring with great exotic sex appeal, but her lack of self-confidence and self-worth attributed to her loneliness. She projected this onto others and you can only attract what you put out.

Angel and Mya had been best friends since forever. As amazing as it seemed, no matter where one was, the other soon followed, thus causing them to maintain a perfect friendship. Both being inherently shy, they were drawn to one another and quickly became a source of strength for each other.

Angel had definitely had a hard time after the death of her fiance, the only man to ever truly appreciate the gift in her. She suffered a nervous breakdown, almost committing suicide and losing all sense of self-respect and self-value. Mya stuck by her side from start to finish, doing what a best friend should do; be there. Angel felt she owed all she was to Mya and their timeless friendship.

Mya couldn't wait to get home. After a day like today, a nice warm house and a hot bath was just what she needed. Mya gathered all her belongings and headed toward the elevator. Of course, the phone rings, but the elevator came, so she headed for it. Oli was on the phone. Not sure what he would say even if she answered, he pretended he was shy but he was going to overcome this phobia for her. The love of his life, although she didn't know it...yet.

Mya hears her phone ringing as she nears the door of her apartment. She has to fumble for her keys and prays the phone keeps ringing until she gets there. Keys, open the door, drop everything, and do the mad dash to the phone just to pick it up on the last ring.

"Hello, hello…"

Angel laughs at her friend as she replays back to her the antics in which she just sped through just to get into the house.

"You know me all too well," Mya admits to Angel as they both crack up with laughter for almost five good minutes. They both wipe away the tears they have shed in the hokey antics of the last few moments. When they are finally able to compose themselves to some level of maturity, they begin to talk for real.

Mya proceeds to tell Angel all about her day from start to finish. Angel is amused but concerned about Mya and Eric. She asks when was the last time she and Eric had a real heart to heart about the status of their relationship. Mya admits they hadn't seen much of each other in at least a month or so.

"If you and Eric aren't careful and mindful of each other, this is the time where things could go real wrong in a relationship. Before you know it, everything is a mess and no one knows when the mess got started…" Angel warns. Mya just listens.

"And be careful of Mr. Hamilton Oliver III. Sometimes things are not what they appear and things that appear to be too good to be true, usually are…" Angel continues. She was concerned because Mya seemed slightly intrigued by this man she doesn't know and doesn't like, or, so she claims. Angel knows better and from what she'd heard on the streets, Eric was a man whore, so Mya would do good finding a side piece or just dropping that bull all together.

Mya counters her barrage of 'mother like statements' with a question of her own.

"Angel, is it so wrong for me to be excited that a man other than Eric finds me attractive?"

"No it's not, but, how many times will men find you attractive and you get excited about it before you do something about the real problem. Your issue is **NOT** men finding you attractive!" Now the fight begins. Mya cannot stand talking to Angel sometimes because she always gets so technical.

"Well, just to let you know…yes, my interest is piqued by this offer from Oli. Hell, why not. It's nice to know I can still turn a head or two every now and then. But, I love Eric and have decided to turn down the offer for dinner…"

"Okay, fine," Angel says perturbed.

"Now what is your problem?" Mya asks, not even really wanting an answer. Angel takes a deep breath and begins to ask her a series of questions.

"Is love enough? Is love enough to make a man or a woman deal with things they would not otherwise deal with from anyone else?" The questions continue. "Is love enough to make it okay to see your significant other only when it is convenient for them? Then only for sex? What exactly is your relationship built on and where is it going?"

Of course, after all this, Mya has no desire to talk to Angel any longer. What she needed was a good chill-out convo with her best friend, not this preachy type of mess.

"Look, I have another call coming through so I'll call you back later…" Angel knows better but agrees to let her go.

Exasperated and a bit depressed, Mya proceeds to draw a bath; nice and hot with bubbles everywhere. After she prepares her giant mug of relaxing herbal tea, she enters the tub. On her small radio, she pops in a CD of smooth jazz, then submerges herself from neck to toe in the water. As the aromatherapy fills the room and her head, Mya puts her head on her bath pillow and closes her eyes. Sleep soon overtakes her and she begins to dream.

BUSINESS LEFT UNFINISHED

She sees Eric, handsome as ever but not with her. He's seated in a lit cafe with a woman…a beautiful woman. She walks in and as she is about to confront them, Oli walks up, looking too good for words. Eric never even looks up, so Mya takes the hint; go with Oli. Mya and Oli go to another restaurant where the ambiance was of love and happiness. They eat good food, drink good wine, and dance the dance of lovers.

Now she is outside glancing into a shop window. She sees Eric again, only this time he sees her as well. She tries the door of the shop but it will not open. Mya sees that woman again dressed only in a slinky, shimmering red teddy. She dances around Eric, playing with his body. Mya finds a brick, hurling it at the picture window. It does not break. Mya is angry! Eric and this woman start kissing, then fade away, mocking her.

Mya almost drowned as the phone rings and scares her out of that blah, blah, blah nightmarish dream. Thank goodness it was a wrong number. Now hotter than her bath water, she wonders if there could be anything to this dream of hers. How would she know? Does she dare call Eric and ask if he's seeing another woman? It certainly wouldn't be the first time. Death would come to her before she ever called Oli.

A cold chill runs through her warm body. Mya knows there is truth to this dream. It may not be true yet, but sure as snow is white, the truth will always come out.

Chapter 6

Skeletons Can Run..Can You?

Eric suddenly awakes feeling as if someone's calling out to him. He sits up in bed, turns on the lamp and peers at his bedside clock. It's only 4:00 a.m. *Mya will kill me for calling her this early but I need to know she's okay.* He takes a deep breath and presses the button with her picture on it. The phone rings twice and Eric is just about to disconnect when a disoriented Mya answers the phone.

"Hey babe…uhm…I woke up feeling kinda funny with you on my mind and I needed to call to make sure you are ok. I'm sorry to called at such an early hour, but I had to be sure…"

Mya yawns deeply before replying, "It's okay. I'm fine and I'll talk to you later today. Go back to sleep…" She hangs up.

Eric breathes a sigh of relief, yet is still somewhat troubled. In his heart, he perceives that something is seriously wrong with this picture. The feeling was like none he'd ever experienced and he sure as hell didn't like it. Not one damn bit. Even with the dirt he was dabbling in, he hadn't expected to get caught up in his feelings like this. It was like some premonition type mess and he wasn't down for that at all.

"What the hell is really going on?" He asked the darkness as he decided to just stay up, take a shower and prepare for his day. Sleep was lost to him at this point anyway.

As he was getting out of bed, the incredible sense of someone needing him gripped him like an iron fist that he couldn't shake. He literally collapsed back onto the bed. Who was this person? Where were they? How could he go to them, how could he help without knowing who or where to go? Then, as suddenly as it had come, it was gone. Just like that...poof! Would he ever know? He was so overwhelmed, he climbed back into bed and just laid there, more than a little spooked and not knowing what to do next.

Autumn was dreaming. The same dream she'd been having for several months now, with increasing frequency.

She is walking down a runway of sorts. In the crowd are the most famous designers and heavy hitters in the fashion world. They are calling her name and applauding. She is the main attraction, the only attraction. In a flash, she slips; her foot is caught in the hem of the beautiful designer original dress she's wearing. As she tumbles out of control, to what seems like her death, no one is even trying to catch her. They all close their eyes and turn their heads. She is screaming but cannot hear herself, so no one else appears to hear her. As she tries one last time to scream at the top of her lungs, she sees her man. Eric is standing right in front of her with open arms. Yet, as she reaches for him, he backs up, mocking her with a deceptive smile. She is in utter disbelief. He continues to move further and further from her grasp, the smile becoming a crescendo of hard laughter, until at last he is like a ghost disappearing into darkening mist. She continues, silently screaming, to fall into the black abyss.

Just before she hits the bottom of nothingness, she awakens with a start, hitting her bedroom floor hard. She is sweat soaked, quite discombobulated and stunned. Had she been screaming aloud? Eric would not do that to her? Would he do that? Of course not! How absurd!

Autumn knows Eric is in a relationship with someone but she cares not. She believes that with all her sexual prowess and never give up attitude, come hell or high water, that man is gonna be hers, and no fake ass, nightmare of a dream is gonna change that!

Chapter 7

Are You Lonely For Me?

Sterling Larson felt like crap. His life hadn't been quite the same since moving to Madison, Wisconsin. He was unsure about his future as it stood with his job, his life and with his woman. Was she still even his? He couldn't expect her to just sit and wait for him to come back; especially since he'd left with not so much as a goodbye or a phone call. They'd known what was coming with this new job but, hadn't expected it all to happen so fast.

He was lonely…bottom line. The kind of lonely beyond the comfort he usually found in the bottom of a glass of white Tequila. He was longing for Angel, yet Angel hadn't thought about him even before he left. Angel didn't even know he still existed.

Sterling had seen Angel one day near his mother's home. She was outside caring for the children at the daycare center. He was captivated by her beauty, the deep darkness of her skin and those penetrating eyes. She was the most gorgeous creature he'd ever laid eyes on in his life. She'd noticed him staring but, of course, she'd dismissed it as just another stranger judging her dark skin and never gave it another thought.

In all honestly, Angel had seen Sterling several times as well and was also smitten by his good looks and beautiful smile. She told herself not to even think about this man. He couldn't possibly be interested in her, but she found herself often daydreaming about him.

Angel's problem was she continued to hold onto the memory of her deceased fiance, making it hard to even address another man. Mya had told her more than once that holding on to him would not bring him back and only make it difficult for her to find love in the arms of another. She knew this to be true, yet, she felt guilty even gazing at Sterling. Like somehow she was being unfaithful to her lost love's memory. So, to think of

BUSINESS LEFT UNFINISHED

Sterling beyond that point was something she had to consciously force from her mind. Fortunately for her, it wasn't working too well.

Sterling seemed to come by about the same time every afternoon, as the kids were outside at recess. One day he got up the nerve to go over to the gate and say hello. Angel almost ran over one of the children getting to him. They were smiling like two giddy middle school kids. This went on for about 4 months, although they never exchanged phone numbers. Angel was unsure of how to deal with the guilt of talking to another man. So she never let Sterling get too close to her emotionally. She just wanted to touch him, to make sure he was real.

However, Sterling was ready for whatever Angel might have to offer him, even though he could sense she was uncomfortable about something. She assured him it had nothing to do with him but didn't give further details.

On one afternoon a few weeks later, he mentioned to her the possibility of a new job in his future.

"I might be moving to Wisconsin soon. There's a job opportunity opening up that I'm sorta interested in..."

Unsure what to say, Angel just cautiously replied, "Well, if it's something you want, I hope you get it...uhm...keep me posted, ok?" The subject was never breached again.

Sure enough, as Angel had just gotten used to expecting to see him every day at the gate, one day he just didn't show. She continued to look for him every day for about a month and then figured the job must have come through. Hurt was written all over her face. *He could have at least said goodbye* she thought, *but who am I? He did not owe me anything, so what difference does it make?* And, that was that. She never mentioned the episode to another soul. Not even her best friend Mya.

"I have no reason to ever think of him again" she told herself but she did. Every day that passed.

So here they were, two people in two completely different places doing the exact same thing; thinking about each other. Thinking of the what if's…the coulda, shoulda…wouldas and regretting never truly being honest with one another about how and what they were feeling.

Sterling was never the guy who got to keep the girl. He was the guy who had the girl but lost the girl to the captain of the football/basketball/baseball or even the chess team. He'd never quite figured out what it was about him that kept him from hanging onto said girl. And, the girls didn't help his case any. They always told Sterling that it wasn't him..well not usually. Most of the breakups went like this:

"Well Sterling, you are a great guy, I just don't like you like that." Or…

THE BOSS LADY

"Sterling, I love being with you but, you are more like a.. you know, like a brother." Uggghhhhh!!! He would rather have wrestled with a bear than to hear that lame excuse one more time.

This man was almost certain his lack of aptitude with the female gender would be his lifelong curse. Hence, his present situation. Maybe he just wasn't attractive enough, or, could it be he wasn't assertive enough? Whatever the case, here we had a successful, articulate, gorgeous man who was afraid of expressing himself to a woman. Maybe his insecurity in that area was his main issue. Especially with the woman of his dreams; the woman he wholehearted believed he loved. The woman he felt he could easily spend the rest of his life with.

Sterling came from two beautiful parents. His mother was a strikingly beautiful woman with strong features. She had intense, piercing hazel colored eyes. That was his favorite thing about his mother. Her skin was smooth as peanut butter; rich and creamy. Strong, high cheek bones made her appear to be smiling if you were standing behind her, even if she wasn't. Her hair was thick, wavy and full of body. Sterling never knew his father and according to his mother, he wasn't missing a lot, but it was obvious, based on his looks, that his dad must have been something special.

Despite his mother's good looks, Sterling wasn't that "pretty boy" kinda good looking. He was just above your average guy, not hard on the eyes but nothing too special. He had a full set of beautiful teeth, hair on his head and was not missing any limbs. He *did* suffer from a mild case of scoliosis, which was a curvature of his spine, but nothing too noticeable. He'd been born with it and came to accept it with no issue. It added to his personality he told himself. He had pointy ears, which the few girlfriends he *did* have thought were so cute. Sterling knew he didn't have a model's beauty but he was also pretty sure he didn't look like a gremlin. He was full of personality, witty jokes and a decent enough smile. That had to be enough for someone..he was hoping it was enough for Angel. However, his one outstanding attribute was his eyes. They were the same piercing hazel as his mother's with green-gold reflects he could only assume must have come to him from his father. It was the eyes that attracted most women. Sadly, they weren't enough to keep those women interested in him, or so he thought. His lack of self-confidence and sense of worth was almost equal to Angel's.

Sterling's mother died when he was at that awkward time in his life. She left him with so many unanswered questions about getting along in the cruel world. She had only begun to teach him the ins and outs of dealing with women and having no real strong male role models, he was left at a loss. It had been an unexpected death and was something he had not yet recovered from. Then entered an Angel; his Angel. She reminded him of his mother in her softness of tone and manner. Sterling would love to have made Angel his girl, his friend, his lover.

He knew he should had made his move on her before he left but had been unsure of how to approach her. Now that he had actually left town without being able to bring Angel with him,

BUSINESS LEFT UNFINISHED

Sterling knew he had to act fast if he wanted Angel to even know what was going on with him. The sense of urgency overcoming him, forced Sterling to think hard to come up with some way to rectify his stupid mistake.

After some serious brainstorming, one evening, Sterling placed an envelope in the mailbox, addressed to Angel at the daycare. He'd written her a brief letter explaining his situation. He then asked her to contact him at the number he provided. He so hoped she'd called, sooner rather than later. The call *would* come, but it would definitely be later...much, much later.

Chapter 8

<u>What The Hell Just Happened?</u>

This was the worst part of her day, the time of day when she was all alone: Dusk, as evening turned into night. Then night into day; the longest hours of her life. But, Angel's life was about to change in what seemed to be a blink of an eye. The way she saw it, it was simple. She blinked once when she met her soul mate, Mr. Right, or her Mr. So-So Wrong. When she blinked again, she couldn't believe her eyes.

This literal tall, dark, and handsome stranger was at the local Pick-N-Pay one Friday evening as she was checking out. He seemed to call to her inner soul; the depth of her being, impacted by the way this man looked at her. He was the color of darkness; three o'clock in the morning with no stars. He had the smoothest skin, it was flawless and his teeth were white as the driven snow.

Those eyes…they were beautiful. A mixture of brown with a hint of green or was it gray in his eyes? They were full of mystery as was Lincoln St. John.

Lincoln was always trying to surprise Angel, either with flowers, jewelry, or a trip somewhere. His love was neither cheap nor wavering for his wife to be; he would do anything for her, anything at all. Even die for her.

Angel spent all her waking moments with him. Never had she known a love like this. They were soul mates, at least that's what they wanted to believe and it seemed as if they would be together forever. Some things just belong together. Peanut butter and jelly, sunny days and bumble bees, cookies and milk; and Lincoln and Angel. Love was all over them and they loved *being* in love.

Thing was, he had issues, demons and skeletons he was running from. He took these fiends with him into every relationship he had. Lincoln St. John was a man with a shady and mysterious past that no one ever got a handle on. Not due to lack of trying, there just never seemed to be any good leads on him. He just appeared out of nowhere, with no past to speak of, as if he just evolved out of the dirt.

He'd grown up on the outskirts of nowhere, real close to goodbye. He was a loner and a troubled man. Born to a crack-head mother and goodness only knows what type of father, Lincoln was bounced from home to home and shelter to shelter most of his young life. He was not liked in most of the places he lived for various reasons. Some founded, most unfounded. There was a general theme that rang true in all cases…he was not sure which team he played on. He had a history of inappropriate behavior, as early as age 7, with one of his female shelter mates. By the age of 9, he had further incidents of the same thing 12 times, only by now, half of his accusers were male.

Lincoln himself was not sure what that meant. He knew he was not supposed to like boys but he just couldn't help himself. His demons took root in his soul. Something was deep inside of him he couldn't fight. He could *not* stop himself when left alone with one of his foster brothers the girls said was cute. He would wait until no one was around before he made his move. He was smooth even as a young boy; he knew what he was doing most of the time. It was usually close to bed time or right after baths before he put his moves on his victim. His move was signature. He would start with small talk, not about anything in particular, just general conversation. His prey would be so caught up in the conversation they never noticed as he had moved closer. He was real casual in placing his hand on a knee or shoulder. Since they were young, the other boy never suspected getting a kiss, especially from his foster brother. This behavior led to many fights, hence solidifying Lincoln's movement through the system.

There were a few instances where his advances were not fought. He was a teenager when he had his first real male on male sexual experience. Only this time, he was not the predator, but the prey. He wasn't completely sure how to feel about it, but when it was all said and done, he did not tell. He did not cry nor did he seem at all surprised that he'd enjoyed it. From what he'd been told, it wasn't right or natural to behave this way. As he'd heard the social workers say, as they tried to place him over and over again, but it felt right at the time for him. He also had his way with the girls because he was so cute or fine, as they said when he was older. He bedded many but was never quite as satisfied as he was when he was "with" the guys.

By his 19th birthday, Lincoln had worn out his welcome at his last group home and set out to find his own way in the world. He had no real job skills but was an excellent painter when inspired and a superb cook. His passion seemed to be causing lots of trouble. Above all else, Lincoln was a perfect criminal; an accomplished thief. Before leaving his last two homes, he made sure he didn't leave empty handed as in previous times. He knew he was nearing the end of his time in the homes for the sexual misconduct, as well as his age. He also knew if he was going to make it out on the streets, he needed cash or at least something he could sell for cash. He hit the jackpot and big! Dude racked up over $20,000.00 in cash and merchandise before they finally put him out. He was okay with that. His final parting gift in both homes was a dozy; their sons had been had…by a man.

Due to his treacherous past, Lincoln had a jealous streak out of this world. It was unfounded in most cases, but when he got an idea in his head, he ran with it. The dirt he'd done in past relationships made it hard for him to trust anybody, even though in 9 out of 10 cases, there was not an issue. There was never any infidelity, man or woman. Lincoln's partners were always faithful because they loved him so. He was sweet as honey dripping off the honeycomb, with the smoothness of a snake and the tricks of a snake charmer. No matter what the sex of his latest conquest, they were loyal to him and loved hard. He just couldn't trust or be trusted because of his own issues and questionable lifestyle. He could, at any given time, be dating up to four people, usually one or two of each and never missing a beat.

THE BOSS LADY

Lincoln believed Angel had been seeing someone else. He certainly was. When and why, she was never sure of, nonetheless, he believed it to be so. He begin to feel she was "acting funny" which is what he used as an out in all his other relationships. The term "acting funny" had its own meaning to him; a plain and simple excuse. If you didn't say "I love you" just right, or didn't respond as you normally would to one of his gestures, you got called out for "acting funny".

Lincoln was insecure in his relationship with Angel just as he'd been in every other relationship he'd ever had but he'd hoped this relationship would be different. He needed it to be different and real. He actually *wanted* to be in love with this woman…any woman, because that would mean he didn't really have a thing for me men. After all, it was just a phase, right? It had to be! He simply could *not* be that way. When he and Angel got hot and heavy, he knew he was "cured". He was all man and didn't have to worry about his past situations. Until that one night…that one, fateful night that changed his life.

Chapter 9

<u>A Whole Heap Of Trouble!</u>

Lincoln had been out all day, doing whatever it was he did all day; nobody ever knew for certain. He'd apparently had a hard day and raced down to **Stinky Pete's Tavern** to get a beer and head to Angel's. Well, one beer turned into a six pack followed by a couple of shots of tequila. He never could handle the tequila, so he knew he could be headed for trouble after his first shot. He started out drinking alone but there was this guy he happened to see that frequented the bar quite a bit and they made eye contact. As guys, they were cordial at first, with head nods or grunts in the other's direction. Neither suspected what would happen next, well at least not Lincoln.

He stumbled into the rest room to get rid of some of that beer. As he came out of the stall to wash his hands, he noticed dude standing in the corner by the urinals. The smile on dude's face was one that Lincoln immediately recognized. That "I want to get with you and I know you want me" type of smile. He'd seen it many times, on many different faces over the years.

Just like that, with no discretion or anything, they were going at it right in the middle of the restroom. They somehow held it together long enough to go to dude's upstairs apartment, then it was ON! Kissing and touching, biting and grunting, with raw animalistic passion…it was unreal. Like something from some hard core porn scene and quite disturbing in its savagery.

After two hours of this wild marathon, Lincoln broke out in a cold sweat…what the hell was he doing? *I cannot be doing this! What am I doing here…oh my goodness…this cannot be happening! Shit! What have I done?*

Angel had been blowing up his cell phone but after 25 missed calls, she said forget it and whisked herself off to bed. How was he going to face her? He did not even know dude's name, let alone anything else about him, except for…well, that was irrelevant. He had just done the one thing he thought he'd gotten over. He had reverted back to his old ways, and to be honest, that shit was good. Of course, because they were both acting like horny dogs, neither of them had thought to use protection.

Lincoln, up to this point, was clean, AIDS testing wise; Angel made sure of that. He'd been nervous about the test because of his lifestyle, not at all sure what the test would reveal. He sweated bullets until the test results came back but she was not giving it up until she knew he was straight. So now what? **NOW WHAT?!**

Lincoln got up so he wouldn't disturb dude, since he didn't even know his damned name. He was so disgusted with himself for letting his demons get the best of him. Or, was it that he just had to get it in like that one more time…just one last time. Okay, but now he needed to get home to his Angel, the woman who could save him from himself, from the evil that lurked in the back of his mind.

It was the wee hours in the morning before he made it home, still reeking of alcohol, sweat and animalistic sex. Angel was sound asleep…good! Angel liked her sleep and if she was asleep, you'd better not wake her unless it was an extreme emergency. Lincoln knew she'd been worried before finally going to bed, so he let her sleep. Plus, he needed a hot shower and some time. He'd be up all night working on his story for tomorrow when he would have to pay the piper.

Chapter 10

King Kong Ain't Got Nothing On Me!

November 11 – Veteran's Day – A day that seemed to last for years to come. The details were a bit fuzzy for Angel. Due to the pain she experienced from recalling the awful event or because it all happened way too fast. She would have rather have forgotten what happened, but that would have been far too easy.

The morning started with Lincoln apologizing with a full course gourmet breakfast. Angel was so tired when she was awakened by the smell of fresh fruit and fresh ground coffee, she felt some of her anger slip away. This always gave away the fact he'd done something he had no business and Angel knew it was beat up. She made her way to the bathroom then down to the kitchen, where she could not believe her eyes.

THE BOSS LADY

The brother had pulled out all the stops. Fresh lilies and carnations adorned a table set with fine china and all the trimmings. Mimosas swam fluid in each wine flute, laced with linen napkins to hold in the coldness, while the carafe rested, chilling on ice. Upon seeing the obvious over-indulgence, Angel was convinced something terrible had taken place; she just wasn't sure she wanted to know what. Lincoln had cooked before for the two of them but Angel had always done the table preparation. This was beyond beautiful and way too much.

The sun shined brightly in the breakfast nook as Angel came down the stairs, catching him by surprise. He looked as if he'd seen a vision, an angel for real, and he didn't like the cold fingers crawling up his back. He couldn't put his finger on it but the feeling of impending doom was strong as hell. Something bad was heading for one of them, he wasn't sure which, but he didn't like it either way.

BUSINESS LEFT UNFINISHED

As Angel prepared to sit at the table, Lincoln rushed to pull her chair out. As he fixed her plate, he made sure everything was to her satisfaction. The shrimp omelet with Swiss cheese, bacon, mushrooms, onions and green peppers, brandished a creamy butter sauce. He'd prepared silver dollar pancakes with fresh strawberries, whipped cream and warmed maple syrup. There was fruit of all kinds, as well as fried potatoes with onions, grilled breakfast steaks, and fresh baked croissants, steaming hot. Angel knew he'd messed up **BIG TIME** with all this lavish spread but there was no sense in ruining the moment. There was *definitely* no benefit in wasting all this delicious food her stomach agreed. So, she smiled her sweetest smile, said good morning and jumped right into her meal. It was the best kind; home-cooked and prepared by one helluva chef.

After finishing, she gave Lincoln a quick peck on the cheek, scurrying offer to shower and dress. Never saying much more than a "thanks for breakfast, it was GREAT!" caused Lincoln to fly into a rage. He was so infuriated, he could have gotten a murder charge. His insecurity kicked into full overdrive. He was totally pissed, with no explanation for it, other than his own wrong doing and f'd up behavior the night before. She had to be sleeping with someone else was the only reason he could give for her seeming lack of irritation and jealousy this morning. Why else would she not say anything? Why? Hell, he was neither dumb nor stupid and neither was she. He was thrown into a state of shock, but what angered him most, was the fear creeping into his bones. What the hell was going on?!

Angel was upstairs glowing in the knowledge of Lincoln stewing downstairs. She knew he was wondering why she hadn't inquired as to his whereabouts from the previous evening, and, she knew he was pissed by that fact. That was just what he deserved for worrying her half the night, then thinking a quick, lavish meal would fix it all. The nerve of this dude! How gullible and stupid did he really think her to be?!

Angel thought she was smart. She'd devised what she thought was a fool proof plan. She'd just make Lincoln feel horrible enough to tell her where he was last night...just spill all the beans. However, this would be the last time she came up with a so-called *fool proof plan*. Sadly, this one was going to blow up right in her face, in the worst way.

Before going to bed the previous night, she'd come up with a few scenarios of reaction based on Lincoln's actions. Due to the current breakfast situation, she quickly decided she would leave the house and let him clean up the kitchen and all the rest of his mess. She knew full well he would be wondering what she was up to, and, based on previous behavior, she knew he would accuse her of "acting funny." As a precautionary measure, she'd already contacted Mya, briefly informing her of the situation and that she would see her soon. So, Angel got dressed and prepared to make her exit.

As soon as she got to the bottom of the stairs, he was in her face. Sometimes, it's hard to tell if a person is genuinely angry, people have become so adapt at masking their feelings but there was no doubt this man was crazy mad…scary mad, but she showed no fear.

"Excuse me Lincoln." And with the calmness in her voice, he almost lost his grip. He grabbed her arm in such a way, it heightened her sense of self-preservation and got her adrenaline pumping. The look in his eyes was wild, vaguely haunted; a look she had never seen before and never intended to see again.

"Let go of me! What the hell is your problem this morning?" She demanded in a icy, calm tone.

"Where the hell you think you going? You ain't said two damn words to me today and you think you leaving this house?" When she didn't respond, his grip became tighter and his questions more insistent.

"I *said* where you going Angel, huh? What's the mofo's name? Is that where you was last night trick?" He was on a roll now and rolling out of control. Unfortunately, he'd triggered something in her that would have been better left untouched. Hands on hips, Angel was ready for his bullshit!

"Where was I?! Where was I Lincoln? Nicca, you trying to flip this shit on me now, right? As I recall Boo, it was you who didn't bring *yo* ass home last night, not me. You may want to check your damn phone because I'm sure there were at least 10 missed calls, all from this number." Angel couldn't believe her ears! This mutha was tripping for real, trying to accuse her of being with someone else to hide his shit!

Lincoln hadn't expected her to be so quick tempered and quick on the draw but what could he do now? He had to keep with the way this was going; he had already gone too far.

"Missed calls my ass Angel! What's that s'pose to mean? You could have had anybody over here calling me…how I know it was you, huh? How the fuck would I know?!" His anger was building to a rage point…so was hers and that wasn't gonna be a good mix!

"Are you freaking kidding me man? If yo black ass would have answered any of those phantom calls, you would have known exactly who was on the other end. So, where the hell were you? That's all you wanted me to ask, so now I've asked and frankly Scarlet, I don't give a rat's ass!"

She yanked her arm from Lincoln's grip, turning to grab her purse and her keys. She knew she needed to get the hell out of there before something bad happened…she could feel it in her bones. She makes it to the garage and starts her car. Just as she was about to shift into reverse, she sees a large object flying towards her. Shit! It's Lincoln, swan diving at her car. **BLAM!** This fool hits the hood with a bang…it was awful. Impulse leads Angel to step on her brakes, sending him rolling off the car. She's so petrified, she believes she just pissed her pants. She was paralyzed with fear and not sure how to proceed.

She carefully checked all her mirrors, doesn't see him, still immobilized by utter terror. She was sure he had some serious injuries but what the hell possessed him to jump off the top rope onto her car like some fucking flying trapeze artist! Damn! That was going to be a mess explaining to the insurance company.

Against her better judgment, what little she had left, she decided to get out of the car to see where the fool was. She was so scared, her heart was palpitating painfully. She took one foot out of the car and immediately felt a hand grab her ankle. His dumb ass was hiding under the car.

"Oh shit!" She screamed, stomping away his hand with her free foot and jumping back into the car. Now she was in an even worse dilemma; she could run him over by moving the car an inch one way or another. So she waited for what seemed like an eternity, until she finally looked in her rear-view mirror and there he was, perched on the back of her car, looking crazy as hell. Then, as if out of some type of sci-fi/horror flick, she watched while he starts punching out her back window with his bare hands. *Oh my goodness*, she thinks, too stunned to say a word.

THE BOSS LADY

The next few minutes would be the worst of her life thus far. She knew if he got in the car he would hurt her, if not kill her, and that was a chance she was not willing to take. With the car still running, Angel floored it. Lincoln crashed into the back window, not through it; however, with one more jolt, he would be in the backseat. She slammed on breaks and he became a human pinball as he bounced off the car. This man must have been having the adrenaline rush of his life because he just wouldn't stop charging the car like a raging bull. He stood in front of the car, bleeding from various places and looking like a man on the threshold of...death's door.

Lincoln took another running start to jump onto the car but, at this point, Angel's fear was quickly melting into something much worse. This craziness was getting on her last nerve and if you know most women, that's not a healthy thing. She reeves the engine, signaling she's had enough of his game and if he wanted to act crazy, she was more than willing to go along. He was so far out of his head there was no coming back for him; this was his

"Training Day" moment. He knew he was going to die, but he was going down fighting and own his own damn terms.

This was certainly one of those "you gotta see it to believe it" moments. It was just something nobody would believe without pictures or video. The noise had attracted the neighbors, everyone pulling out smart phones instead of dialing 911. The ghetto paparazzi was out in full force. Ms. Johnson, the neighborhood snoop, with her signature pink sponge rollers and those awful pink fuzzy slippers, was leading the pack. After about ten minutes of spectating, she was the first to call the police because that's what she does. She was neighborhood watch for the entire three block radius. Amazing thing was, whenever she called, no matter the complaint, the police were in route, post haste.

Mr. Michelson was just as bad, if not worse. He hated everybody and wanted the whole world in jail, so they would stay off his grass. He'd been Angel's neighbor since she bought her house and he hated her. She spoke one morning, as decent neighbors do, and that was it; he wanted her gone. *Well, now was his chance,* he thought, as he moseyed to the scene with phone in hand, calling the police.

The Mings lived across the street with their hi-tech vlogging cameras. They would have more coverage than the news station, which had not yet arrived. Rest assured they were on their way. Mr. Obadiah worked for somebody, who knew somebody. Somebody who owned something that had a friend who worked for one of the local news channels. He must not have been home; otherwise their cameras would have been everywhere, as the finale was just about to take place.

Angel was now in a state. Not truly grasping what was happening but watching it unfold at the same time. Knowing it was real, yet so unreal and certain the outcome was ***not*** going to be pleasant. Lincoln was still standing upright; he should have been face down in the dirt by now, shouldn't he? With all the injuries he had sustained from his fight with the car, he should have been laid out by now. But, he was like a mad animal and it was too much for words. He was stalking towards her, like some agitated panther, looking right through her, at some invisible foe. She was crying, screaming for him to calm down and just talk to her. How she'd ended up outside the car, she wasn't sure.

"You can't talk to a ghost," he screams back "…you can't talk to somebody who's not here. Lincoln is not here, never was…" Angel wanted to believe it was just part of his "craziness" kicking into overdrive yet something deep in her soul told her otherwise and that he had just spoken his last words.

He came running at her, hands outstretched as if he would choke her, with that wild, maniacal look that was more terrifying than anything. Angel was no fool and took off running back to her car. She was in just when he crashed into the driver's door. She proceeded to put the car in drive, and here is where future accounts get a little fuzzy.

THE BOSS LADY

She swears she puts the car in drive, when in actuality, she put it in reverse and gunned it. Lincoln was now standing off to the side of the car, knowing he has to end this mayhem and finally put the demons to rest. Send them to the same hell they had put him through all these years. He side-steps to the right, putting himself directly in the path of the car. Angel realized what he was doing and tried with urgency to avoid. Too late, way too late! The impact was loud and awful. She comes to a screeching halt, getting the car under control. As she turns to head back in the opposite direction, out of nowhere, Lincoln does another flying leap onto the hood of her car.

"Shit, Lincoln! Cut it out!" She screamed, as she drives with caution and then steps on the breaks, hard. He rolls of and comes right back for more. Angel is distraught, frightened, mad and getting a little fed up with all this foolishness.

"Dammit, you wanna die, let's do the damn thang," she taunted, from the supposed safety of the car. He was coming for her yet, this time without much vigor because he's hurting mentally and physically. He's wounded, battered and bruised but simply cannot stop himself. Angel is a wreck, just wanting this to end. She put the car in park and just put her head on the steering wheel, sobbing without reserve. That's when the shit hit the fan. Lincoln was serious about ending this shit; so he did the only thing he could do.

Knowing that at her worse, Angel deserved much better than what he had to offer, in his broken mind, he was doing her a favor. He stopped right in front of her car, pulled out the hunting knife he often carried, looked her right in her eyes and without another word, slit his throat. As he stood there, blood oozing from the gaping wound, he mouthed his last words to her.

"I love you and I'm so very sorry…"

Angel screamed! The most horrific scream many of her neighbors had ever heard. It was about this time that the faint wailing of the emergency vehicles could be heard, but it didn't matter...nothing really mattered now. Angel was out of the car, cradling Lincoln's blood covered head in her lap as he lay dying in the street by his own hand. There was nothing she could do. He had accomplished just what he'd set out to achieve...slaying the demons in his mind and the one in his pants.

As the sirens drew near, Angel started to drift away. Drift into a place where she had never gone before, she was not sure where it was, but it was warm there. There were no sinister things going on there, just soft lights and warmth. She could hear the sounds behind her. With a quick jolt, she was brought back to the harsh reality of her life.

Suddenly, she was thrust amid the chaos, the lights, the people and massive amounts of blood. So much blood, oh my goodness. Lincoln! Oh shit...ohh shitttt! What the... how had it come to this? What the hell had gone so wrong here? Angel started to vomit.

BUSINESS LEFT UNFINISHED

"My head! Oh shit, I can't see! Lincoln why…why, why whyyyy…" Graciously, the darkness took her and she welcomed it.

When Angel woke, two days later, she was in the hospital. She woke with such a start , Mya almost jumped out of her chair. She'd received a call from the hospital about ten minutes after Angel's arrival, seeing as her name was listed as Angel's first emergency contact. She'd been constantly at Angel's bedside for what seemed like the longest two days of her life. Angel had been sedated from the time they brought her in; she'd been a raving loon once she regained consciousness in the ambulance. She was screaming and fighting the paramedics as she tried to get back to Lincoln.. She didn't want him to be alone, dead as he was.

The months following the funeral were dark, sad, and lonely for Angel. She didn't want to sleep due to the horrible nightmares. She would stay awake for days at a time until she'd finally collapse but the sleep wasn't restful. The bloody images of that awful day forever burned in her brain. Even if she closed her eyes to sneeze or yawn, she would catch glimpses of the madness, the gaping, bloody wound and the mask of a man that now haunted her.

Angel had become a self-imposed recluse. She didn't want any contact with people looking at her like she needed their pity. She did not want anybody's pity; it couldn't compare with her own. She did not leave her house for months; at least no one saw her leave. She didn't answer the phone and she wouldn't let anyone in. Her sister tried to talk with her but to no avail; she wasn't interested in any speeches or pep talks. Mya thought she was the big gun but Angel squashed all that by hanging up on her, disconnecting the phone and the doorbell. Saying, I didn't hear my phone ring or the doorbell, was actually not a lie.

Her mind ran to random thoughts of suicide often. Thankfully, she was too scared to go through with it but she thought about it; a lot. She was so lonely without Lincoln, yet so furious with him for leaving her, especially the way he did.

So, she fell into that dark place that held dark memories and even darker thoughts. It's that deep, dark place within all of us. That place we retreat to when life deals us a hand we can't play or fold on. It was scary but she was okay with that as long as she was by herself and didn't have to deal with anyone else.

So off she escaped, to the only place where it was safe, if only for a little while, she would stay just to regroup. *Yeah, regroup.. that's what I need to do,* she thought. So she jumped in her car and off she rode, with no real direction in mind. She would drive until she got tired, then rent a room for a week or so, and just be…yeah, just be.

However Mya, completely unaware of Angel's plans, had already decided on an intervention, totally disregarding the fact that Angel had told her to mind her own damn business. She attributed Angel's attitude to her feelings and just knew she didn't mean what she was saying. Unfortunately, Mya wasn't high on patience. It certainly wasn't one of her many virtues and she was losing what little she had with her friend. Mya was somewhat bossy but, like most bossy folk, somehow failed to see it…unless it was in her favor. Early on a Saturday morning, some six months after Lincoln's death, Mya made an executive decision to go over to Angel's and make her talk. Okay…good luck with that.

Chapter 11

More Than I Bargained For

Mya arrived at Angel's only to find Angel absent. *Just my luck,* Mya thinks. She was kind of glad Angel wasn't home since her intervention gas tank had already begun to run low. Angel didn't have her cell phone on, which started to worry her a bit. Angel always kept her phone on.

Since she was there and Angel was not, she decided to go in and see if there was any hint as to her best friend's whereabouts. She collected the mail, which was all over the porch and opened the door. The mail signified an absence of at least a few days, which really concerned Mya. *Where the hell is this chick?*

The stench of garbage, and something dead, assaulted Mya's nostrils as soon as she opened the door. There were flies everywhere and her initial feeling was one of horror. She rushed through the house, praying she wouldn't find the terrible scene playing out in her mind. To her immense relief, there was no dead or dying body of Angel in any room and soon Mya found the source of the awful smell…the kitchen. Garbage was piled high against the back door, left overs clung to pots and dirty dishes, and there were even a couple of dead rats reposing in the midst of all the mess. She just shook her head in disgust, knowing what she had to do. She was prepared, although the condition of the place was truly unexpected. When you plan a surprise intervention, you never know what you might find.

She went back to her car and suited up. Several nosey neighbors saw Mya in her get up and grew immediately concerned. They thought she belonged to a hazardous waste or CDC unit and wondered if there was something amiss in Angel's house. One of the neighbors, who'd witnessed the entire sad episode with Lincoln, actually came over to inquire, informing Mya that it had been at least a week since she'd seen Angel's car at the house.

BUSINESS LEFT UNFINISHED

While it was none of their business, Mya explained that Angel was on a long overdue vacation and she was there to give the house a much needed cleaning. The neighbor wishes Mya luck and runs back to her own home.

As Mya re-entered the kitchen, she was threw up. The smell was horrendous, the flies and maggots disgusting and we won't mention the dead rats too much. Thank goodness for the mask she'd had in her car or this job wouldn't get done. She went to work. The garbage had to go!

Opening every window and door to relieve some of the stench, Mya set to getting rid of the mound of garbage. It all had to be double bagged. She almost lost her breakfast again while bagging up the rats. *Shit, I didn't sign up for all this*, Mya thought to herself.

With garbage bagged and removed, she headed for the sink and the pile of dishes and dirty pots. The worse of these Mya didn't even bother trying to wash; they were bagged and readied for the dumpster. What could be washed, was placed in boiling hot, soapy water with a healthy splash of Clorox then rinsed and rewashed in the dishwasher. She then did a complete wipe down from the cabinets to the counter tops with Clorox and pine-sol. The refrigerator, which was just about bare, had a few science projects growing in there that needed to be tossed but was otherwise clean. The stove top was surprisingly clean, yet the oven needed a little work.

With trash removed, dishes clean, every surface wiped down and sparkling, Mya tackles the kitchen floor. She didn't even want to imagine what had caused all the sticky gunk clinging to the tile.

Standing back inspecting her work, Mya was satisfied, lighting a candle to signal a job well done and the help with the lingering smell. The rest of the house wasn't bad at all. Just some minor dusting and vacuuming to bring it all together. She did a mild clean up in Angel's bedroom and bath, nothing spectacular was needed, except to wash all those dirty clothes Angel had just thrown about, and her job was complete. Some five hours later, she was ready to get the hell out of there.

Chapter 12

<u>But Wait, There's More!</u>

Mya leaves Angel's house still concerned, puzzled and starving. The chick still wasn't answering her phone and the house had held no tell-tale signs of where she might be. Mya had contacted Angel's sister in hopes she knew her whereabouts, but that too was a dead end. Now the sister was equally worried. *Where the hell are you girl*, Mya wondered, as she inched her way in the Wendy's drive-thru line. She said a silent prayer for her best friend as she headed home.

While taking a bathroom break, her phone went off, so she rushed out to not miss the call. When she got to the phone, there was no missed call but rather a text message. The number the message came from was not one Mya recognized and the message was just cryptic. It read:

*No worries friend, all is well...*The call back number wasn't accepting incoming calls, so she was stumped. It was a rather creepy message and not much Angel's style at all. Mya forced herself to think positive thoughts. Otherwise, she would have been calling the authorities saying Angel had gone missing with no real proof of that.

With a full stomach and tired from the vigorous clean up, Mya drifted off to sleep...she dreams.

From a distance, she hears Angel calling her in a panic. She goes through a labyrinth of rooms and each room had a picture of Angel, Lincoln, Eric and this strange woman; a woman that is familiar yet not familiar at the same time. She knows she has seen this woman before but she cannot quite place her. The rooms all look the same except for the pictures. The pictures vary from room to room and they get more twisted with each view. The new pictures show Eric and this mystery woman. From one picture to the next, it appears this woman is

Eric's wife. A few of the pictures are wedding photos, with Angel and Lincoln as members of the wedding party. How could that be? Where am I…I should be Eric's wife…what is going on?

As the maze grows more and more abstruse, Mya is not able to find her way and gets lost. The maze becomes more complex, adding dimensions as the rooms get smaller. She is now in a box with the walls closing in, the air getting thin and Mya not being able to catch her breath. She panics, hyperventilating, and then there's a loud crash!

She wakes up on the floor, the crash was the sound of her plate shattering. There is glass everywhere and Mya is now a bundle of nerves…*Who was that woman? What does this dream mean?*

Chapter 13

<u>The Hell You Say!</u>

With all the drama with Angel, Eric got moved to the back burner; however, he was patient and understanding of Mya's situation and her dedication to her friend. Although, he was nearing the end of being a nice guy and had options, he didn't want to use them. He liked the fact he'd kept a few secret loopholes in this relationship with Lady Mya.

He was relaxing in his favorite armchair, thinking about his future. The burning question was, would Mya have play a role in this future? The more intriguing question was, would Autumn would be a part of that future as well?

As he became more open to exploring that option, he felt a little twinge of guilt. He knew he shouldn't but curiosity was getting the best of him. Autumn was a beautiful woman and it was obvious she wanted him.

THE BOSS LADY

The ringing of the phone startled Eric a bit and he smiled when he saw who was calling. He decides to let the call go to voicemail out of childish spite. Thus was the beginning of the little game Eric liked to play. Who would call whom first? She'd been the first to call, but Eric knew he would eventually lose the game, as he often did, so he just called her back. In reality, she *was* simply returning his initial call.

They exchanged pleasantries, how was your day, blah, blah, blah, then Mya got down to the real reason for her call. She caught him completely off guard by asking..

"So, who have you been sleeping with lately?" Eric was shocked she would ask him such a question, although it wasn't like he hadn't done it before. His breathing quickened as did his heart-rate but he remained outwardly composed. *What did she **think** she knew*, he asked himself before answering.

"No one Mya. Currently, I'm not sleeping with anyone, including my so-called girlfriend." Two could play this little game.

"You know what baby, it's not like I'm some ugly dude… I do have options here. If you're not willing *or* able to do your part in this so called relationship, there is this one chick sweating me real hard and I would hate to feel as though you're pushing me into the arms of another." He hadn't planned to go that far but once he got started, he was on a roll.

"…She's been after me for awhile but I've been avoiding her like AIDS because of what I thought we had. Am I making a mistake or what Mya? You tell me…"

Suspicions confirmed by his own words, Mya thought to herself, *so there is another woman involved!* Not only was she in utter disbelief at what Eric had just said, her feelings were hurt to the nth degree. She thought she just might cry but refused to give the idiot that satisfaction.

For a full twenty minute tirade, Mya was respectful, allowing him to get all his feelings off of his chest, and, from the way he was carrying on, he had a lot to get off.

THE BOSS LADY

Once finished, he knew he'd said too much and had showed his hand as well as his ass. Understanding he had sealed his fate with Mya, at this juncture, he was okay with it…for now. He was also smart enough to know Mya was taking all this in and would have something to say about every little thing he'd addressed. Strange thing is, Mya surprised the hell out of him and even herself with her response.

"Eric, I have listened for the last 20 minutes, taking all your concerns into consideration. I love you very much, but I also love me *and* you enough to let you go if that's what it comes down to. Before I make any decisions or comments, I'm going to hang up, do some thinking and talk with you later." With that, she hung up the phone.

Eric looked at the phone like it was an alien. In the entire time he and Mya had been together, she'd never just hung up on him. They'd had many fights, some severe enough to make them not talk for weeks at a time, but never a hang up call. The upside to fighting was, of course, the make-up sex. Now that was worth the fight! Almost always, no matter what the fight, the make up sex made you forget…at least for a little while. But, how does a hang up call end in some good, ole fashioned make up sex?

Mya wasn't sure how she felt about this new turn of events with Eric. She was numb, which wasn't really good or bad. However, she did know she had some issues to work out within herself concerning this so-called relationship.

"Exactly what *am* I going to do? How do I begin to fix this mess? Is there even a fix for this mess? And, if so, the better question is…do I *want* to fix it?" She pondered these questions aloud as she thought about Angel and her current mess. She heads to the kitchen to get her favorite sedative, a glass of red wine. If a glass of this liquid gold couldn't help, there simply was no fix.

After drinking the entire bottle of wine, Mya was still numb and unsure as to how she was feeling. The second bottle of wine brought some peace and tranquility, along with an onslaught of tears that flowed without any effort on her part and didn't stop until they were quite ready. She cried these silent tears for about an hour.

Suddenly, the tears stopped, the true pain surfaced and Mya experienced a hurt like never before; not even the couple of times she'd caught him cheating. This was something on a totally different scale. She had never loved a man like she loved Eric but she knew he was right in his feelings. She wasn't doing all she could or *should* be as a girlfriend. She also knew Eric would break up with her before he broke her heart again. Or, at least she hoped that would be the case.

Chapter 14

I Will Not Be Ignored

Autumn decided the best way to take her mind off Eric was to do something; anything. Few people knew Autumn loved to bowl; she was damn good too. She bowled for two different leagues and had two rings to show for it. There was a bowling tournament going on in Indianapolis, so she decided to go. The situation with Eric was bringing her down; an outlet for her frustrations was what she needed.

Autumn took a moment to reflect over her life, realizing she was pretty satisfied. It was a bonus when things worked out the way she wanted on her terms, but she was a schemer and a devious one at that. She wanted Eric, in every sense of the word and she had the wherewithal to make that a priority.

THE BOSS LADY

Eric had seen her on occasion but never thought of pursuing a relationship with her. He was in love with Mya or so he wanted all to believe. He never seriously thought of entering into a real relationship with anyone else. The casual side fling was one thing…never anything serious or lasting. Yet, she had all but thrown herself at him when she saw him for a third time in her store. It was an odd set of circumstances that brought him to the store to begin with.

He'd been looking for a unique birthday present for Mya, knowing he would find something in there quite special. Eric had heard from Angel that there was an outfit in the store Mya had hinted at about 20 or 30 times. It was a sexy outfit Angel knew he would love and would be perfect for an event they were due to attend in August. Eric, being in touch with his woman, learned all the details, setting out on a mission. She would have that outfit before nightfall.

BUSINESS LEFT UNFINISHED

He'd been in the little shop on Euclid several times. On his first trip, he noticed a beautiful young woman that was later pointed out to be the owner. She was cute and even a little sexy but not for him; not right now. However, the several looks she gave him made it clear she was interested, so, he tucked her safely away in the options part of his brain.

When Autumn saw him, she was certain God had heard her prayers and he was the answer. Sweet. *Thank you Lord! You knew just what I needed...*She couldn't have been more helpful to Eric if her life depended on it She brought out all the stops to impress this man; all the colors, accessories, the whole nine. Not only was she going to make this sale, she was going to make this mission personal. She was going to sell herself as well.

Even after the initial meeting and all the personal attention, Eric decided not to buy the outfit that day. Maybe for a chance to return, perhaps? Even if that were true, it wasn't something he would readily admit. It would be his little secret.

But a determined, head strong Autumn was not to be deterred, not by a long shot. She was certain the next time she saw this man, and there would be a next time, she would make something happen. She would get him to do more than just notice her. She was going to make her move and he was going to acknowledge her.

Eric walked in to the store one day on his lunch break, not to buy anything but, maybe just to see "her". He knew delivery of new merchandise came on Wednesdays and so it was early afternoon on Thursday when he made his appearance. It was like a dream when he came in that day.

Autumn had been having a mediocre day and needed a little pick me up...then *he* walked in. The way the sun was shining through the door made it seem like one of those movie scenes. He came in with a halo and she knew, once again, that her prayers had not fallen on deaf ears. He pretended to be interested in a new men's suits that had just arrived but it appeared his size wasn't on the rack. He used the size issue as an excuse to engage her in conversation and she was all for it. A proper introduction was in order.

"Hello there…welcome back. Yes, I remembered. Let me introduce myself…my name is Autumn Matthews and I own this little shop…" She then extended a dainty, perfectly manicured hand for him to shake. She flirt in her was on 12 out of 10.

He took it, responding, "Hello, I'm Eric McGhee and I like your little shop. Thanks for remembering."

The touch was like electricity to Autumn, yet Eric seemed unaffected, so she plowed forward.

"Not only do I want to help you get this suit in your size, I also desire to get to know you better. You appear to be a very interesting man." There, she'd said it. He just stood there, mouth agape, caught completely off guard by her bluntness. For some odd reason, it rubbed him the wrong way and he let her know this, gently yet firmly.

"Well…uhm…while I appreciate your honesty, I'm really not interested in getting anything but this suit if you can get it in my size". She did not take rejection well at all. She wasn't happy and it showed but she did take Eric's measurements, promising order it in his size and give him a call when it came it. He gave her his business contact, they exchanged a few more pleasantries and he departed.

Autumn was so pissed after he left, she closed shop for the day. On her way home, she stopped by the store to pick up a few things, mostly wine. Little Penguin wine, in every flavor. She was planning a party and she was the only invitee. She was despondent; just shocked he would dismiss her that way. He had some nerve! Who in the hell did he think he was talking to?! She planned to give him a mouthful when he came in to pick up for his suit.

BUSINESS LEFT UNFINISHED

What Eric didn't know is that the perfect fitting suit was already available in the stock room. She was taking this week to cook up a scheme to get in his head, or his pants, whichever came first. She was drunk by the end of the second bottle, feeling no pain. She'd just happened to bring home his order form, only his, and was debating if she should call him. *What the hell,* she figured, *what could it hurt?* She blocked her number through caller id just in case he didn't answer or some mysterious female did.

Just as the phone started ringing, she got spooked and hung up. *Come on Autumn,* she coaxed herself, *what are you afraid of? You have never been afraid of any man, no matter how good looking or his status was.* So, she picked up the phone, dialing again. This time she let it ring, and this time, he picked up, but she froze. Panicking, she dropped the phone, then hurried hung up.

Eric found it odd, he didn't receive many prank calls and two in one night bothered him. He wasn't shaken or rattled often but, nonetheless, he was curious. Plus, that experience a few nights pass still had him a bit apprehensive. He punched in *69, but with no luck; the number was private. Of course it was. He shook it off, already in bed and ready for a good night's sleep. He'd had a busy day at work and was expecting an even busier one tomorrow. He soon drifted off to sleep, but there was no rest. Dreams taunted his mind, endless visions of Mya, and this other woman.

They were arguing and he wasn't sure what to do. As he approached them, they both turned to face him, laughing in his face; this was disturbing. Various visions included he and Mya on an island where she becomes an attack victim of a shark. Upon closer inspection, it was not a shark, it was this other woman with wicked teeth and sharp razor like hands ripping Mya to shreds. Eric jumped, but did not awaken and the next vision was just as disturbing.

Eric and Mya were getting married, but this was no ordinary wedding or dream, for that matter. Eric was standing at the end of a red carpet, at the altar waiting for her to walk down the aisle. With gale force wind, the doors of the church fly open and there was this woman again, dressed in a wedding gown, screaming that Eric would be marrying her, not Mya. This sends the church into an uproar with parents fainting and bridesmaids demanding to know what the hell was going on. Then, as if this wasn't disaster enough, Mya comes down the aisle, soaked from head to toe, in some awful brown substance. It was nasty and stank to high heaven. Whatever this substance was, it was thick and the color of dried blood, but the smell was terrible. She was trying to scream, holding her neck but, as she got closer, Eric noticed a gaping wound at her throat. He becomes physically ill, in his dream and in real life, as he starts to vomit.

He jolts awake, in time to make it to the bathroom, shaking uncontrollably. *What the hell was that,* he thinks, as he spills the contents of his gut into the toilet. *I have to call Mya,* was his next urgent thought. *I gotta make sure she's was okay…*One ring, two rings, three rings…voicemail. He wasn't good with that at all.

There was only one thing left to do, take a ride. He was wide awake now and still shaking, sweat beads forming all over his body to cool his overheated skin.

Twenty minutes later, as he pulled into Mya's driveway, he noticed something unsettling. It appeared her front door was open and all the lights were on. Now he was really freaked out. He parked with abandonment, the car still rolling as he jumped out and ran into the house. He completely forgets the rules of common sense, rushing in with no caution whatsoever. He went storming in yelling and screaming for Mya; she was not there.

Where the hell could she be? It's 3:30 in the morning and she is not home. Eric stopped long enough to take a look around. There was nothing out of place, the house was clean. Okay so, there had been no murder here but where was she? He called her cell phone, which he hadn't bothered to do earlier, since he figured she would be home sleep.

BUSINESS LEFT UNFINISHED

Just then there was a thump, nothing major but enough to grab his attention. He was in such a state, he couldn't figure out where it came from. He stopped, nothing…until a few seconds later when he heard it again. This time it was more like a thud and it was coming from the attic.

There were two rooms in any house he despised, the basement and the attic. The thought of having to go into either of these was causing a panic attack. There was a deep trauma connected to his past that caused the apprehension over these rooms. *But, why in the hell would Mya be in the attic? She don't even like going up there for Christmas decorations!*

Eric made his way back to the hallway, heading for the attic space. He noticed the ladder was down but the door wasn't open. He hears the sound again, much louder this time. By now, he's sweating bullets, as he pushes open the overhead door and prepares himself for the worse. He felt something scurry across his arm, screamed, dropped the door back in place with a loud bang, and almost fell off the ladder.

"Get yourself together man!" He whispers with anger as he plunges head first into the attic darkness.

All he found was a family of birds. The thud was the sound of the attic window being pushed against the wall by the wind. There was no sign of Mya or anything suspicious. But, where the hell is she...

———————————

Angel grew weary in her seat, deciding to stretch her legs a bit. She'd never been a fan airplanes but this was the quickest way to her destination. She couldn't wait. She couldn't pinpoint the last time she was this excited about anything.

In retrospect, Angel thought her relationship with Lincoln had been wonderful. It had started out so great, like a true love story and even up to the end. She still, in some ways, believed he'd been her soul mate. Coming to terms with the reality of his death and the tragedy of it all hadn't been easy, but she was finally ready to move on with her life. Lincoln's decision to kill himself had been his alone and she refused to continue to bare the weight of it.

See, Angel was on the hunt; the hunt for the one person she believed could help her make sense of her life. Sterling. She knew the only way to handle this was to just take the bull by the horns and let the chips fall where they may. She also knew better than to tell Mya because she would only try to stop her.

She'd received Sterling's letter a couple of weeks after meeting Lincoln, stashing it in her bedside draw because she believed she'd *met* the love of her life. Something, call it divine providence if you wish, prompted her to retrieve the letter before she left for parts unknown. Over the course of the month she was gone, she read it several times, picked up the phone several times to call him and immediately hung up before he could answer.

THE BOSS LADY

When she'd finally built up enough nerve to speak to him, the conversation that followed was short but very sweet.

"Hello..." she almost hung up again but rushed forward before she lost her nerve completely.

"Hel...uhm...hello..." she cleared her throat of the lump forming. "Is this Sterling Larson?"

Sterling smiles on the other end, recognizing her voice immediately. *It took you long enough*, he thinks to himself before confirming.

"It is and who do I have the pleasure of speaking with?" Angel breathed a huge sigh of relief, hearing the near laughter in the way he'd posed that question. It was gonna be okay.

"Hi Sterling, it's Angel. How have you been? Sorry it took me so long to contact you but a lot has been going on..." She let her words trail off, not sure how much she should reveal before she knew what he would do next. His reply pleasantly surprised her, setting the tone for the rest of the conversation.

"To be honest with you Angel, I'm shocked you called at all, considering the way I left without so much as a goodbye. Chuck it up to my stupidity and insecurity and let's start right here. It's good to hear your voice…"

Now she was on her way, going halfway across the country to see someone she didn't really know. She'd never even contemplated doing anything like this, but she'd wasted enough time hurting and being alone. Maybe it was love, pure and simple, and took a tragedy to make her realize what had been in front of her the whole time. Either way, Angel was determined to find out what really existed between she and Sterling.

However, Sterling was in a bit of a pickle. After all this time, the woman of his dreams was on her way to see him. He was over the moon but, his current girlfriend, may not feel quite the same.

THE BOSS LADY

He'd decided to move on with his life, well sort of, after months of not hearing anything from her. Enough time passed that Sterling felt he owed it to himself to look for a companion or at least a long term booty call, if you will. Yet, unlike most men, Sterling made it crystal clear to whomever he was seeing that it was just a temporary fix. He was a hopeless romantic and believed Angel would somehow find her way to him. When *that* happened, it would be over with the other woman...point, blank, PERIOD.

There were some good dates and some he thought he might have to call the police on. Few of the women he met were receptive to the idea of just being a booty call, but there were a couple who were just looking for someone to pass time with them as well. All in all, he'd kept it honest from the start.

Now he had to end it with this woman, who he kind of liked, but she was no Angel; not his Angel anyway. She should be arriving soon and there was really no sense in prolonging the inevitable. Like the ones before her, she'd known well ahead of time what she was getting into and had agreed.

Just as she got to his door, the phone rang. Sterling opened it, then rushed to answer the phone. By his tone and body language, **current situation** knew her time was up. She didn't make a sound as she wrote Sterling a little note saying thanks for the memories…and left. That's how you play the game ladies and gents! Arrive with dignity and class…leave with dignity and class.

Sterling was so excited, he almost forgot she'd been there. He found the note sometime later, almost feeling bad, but as he threw it in the trash, he realized he couldn't have been happier. He tidied up his place then headed off to the train station to meet Angel.

Making it from the airport to the train station had been a bit of a hassle but she was finally seated, allowing her nerves to calm and her mind to relax. *I just can't believe I'm here,* was her only thought, as the train jostled her back and forth. Her journey was almost over. She was on her way to reunite with the man whom she believed could give her a reason to live again.

This was her first experience on a train, and what an experience it was. There were quite a few characters on board, and the one that sat next to her decided he would take their relationship to the next level by rubbing her thigh. As she smiled that big doe eyed smile of hers then punched him in the nose, he knew it wouldn't work out between them. No real surprise there.

By the time they reached her stop, she was again a bundle of nerves; the butterflies more like birds flying around in her stomach. She had a million and one questions floating around her head. *Will he even recognize me? Will I him? Do I even know what the hell I'm doing?!*

Sterling was waiting for his future wife, *at least she better be*, at the Miles Avenue train station. He was a nervous wreck. He had a picture so he would know her as soon as she stepped off the train, but in retrospect, those eyes were something no one could ever forget. She told him her hair color change and that she had lost few pounds but nothing prepared him for what he saw.

As the trains pulled in, the doors opened, and hundreds of people flooded the platforms; none of them was his Angel. He scanned the pic in his hand against the faces before him but just did not see her. *Had she changed her mind? Did she somehow miss her train?*

Just as Sterling was about to panic, there she was, like a vision from a dream. He almost choked at the vision of beauty standing so alive in front him. She was beautiful in every way possible. Neither could believe she was there, standing there…with him, with her…together. It felt right…it felt good.

They gazed into each other's eyes, searching for certainty and needing the unspoken validation. The answers to all questions was find there, in the windows to their souls. Tears flowed freely in their eyes, cleansing the souls of two people who had been through so much, lost so much and yet found so much more. In unison, they moved closer to wipe away the other's tears and collapsed into one another's arms.

After what seemed like an eternity just holding one another, they finally gathered Angel's bags, heading out of the train station. After loading the car, some dinner was the next order of business. There was a great seafood joint right around the corner, so they decided to have their first meal as a couple there. It all seemed so surreal to Angel, she couldn't keep it to herself.

"Sterling, this is so amazing and unbelievable all at the same time. I've left my comfort zone to travel far and way beyond anything I've ever done before. Could you pinch me so I'll know I'm not dreaming?!" Sterling reached over laughingly to give her a little pinch…she yelped happily.

"I have no problem with that whatsoever and, no…you're not dreaming. At least I hope not 'cause if you *are* then that means I am too and I need this to be as real as anything in my life has ever been…" He then grasped her hand, entwining their fingers tightly together. He had her now and he sure as hell wasn't letting go. She smiled shyly, continuing to give voice to her thoughts.

"First, I need you to be completely honest with me, now and forever. The one thing I don't think I could handle is secrets. No matter what it is or how bad you may *think* it is, imma need you to trust me enough to tell me the truth. Secondly, I need you to love me with all you have and more importantly, be patient with me. I still have some things within that I may need to work out…"

Sterling just stared at her. In awe that this beautiful being was there with **him**, wanting **him**, had come all this way for **him**, in love with **him;** wanting to be with **HIM**. He was like a man who'd just won the lottery! He had to compose himself before he spoke. Who would have thought he'd be experiencing a dream come true moment in the parking lot of the Crab Shack Seafood Hut in Madison, Wisconsin? *She said she wanted complete honesty, well, here goes…*

THE BOSS LADY

"Angel, from the first day I laid eyes on you, I knew in my heart you were the one for me. Sure, it took a while, there were obstacles and circumstances to get over, but here we are. I believe what God predestines for us is sure to be, no matter how long it seems to take. My love for you will never be in question. I loved you when I didn't even know your name. The time we spent apart finding our way back to one another only made my love for you grow. ***That's*** how I know it's real. No matter what relationship I was in, it was just to pass the time while I waited for what I knew God had for me...you. You have me, ***all*** of me without question, for as long as you want me..." Silence.

Emotions ran too high for words at that moment. But then, it had all been said. It was becoming more and more clear there was a bigger plan at work here. They both surrendered to the invisible, yet awesome power operating within them...Love. They were finally free to live in lightheartedness, peace, joy, self-confidence and a sense of self-worth and value that only comes from knowing and loving oneself with God's abundant love.

BUSINESS LEFT UNFINISHED

Angel was in heaven; the journey through hell, bringing her to her proper place at last. Sterling was as happy as a boy in a store with his favorite candy…his chocolate covered angel with the big, beautiful eyes.

 *Chapter 15*

<u>Final Breaking Point</u>

Mya had had enough! She was making a move she never thought she would make, going to see Oli. She'd decided to only have minimal contact with him, if for no other reason, than to piss him off. Truth be told, she was really interested in Oli and they both knew it. On a few occasions, she'd even called Oli at work, pretending to need legal advice and found herself leaning on him for support during Angel's ordeal. He had become her rock, although he didn't know this. He was kind and quite easy to talk to once you got to know him; not the conceited jackass everyone thought him to be on first impression.

The Eating Spot was famous for its chicken salad and those tasty, tangy wings. Tuesdays was wing day, so Mya skipped over to the 731 Building, Oli's building, to have her a little lunch and a peek. She never approached him during these clandestine lunches and she doubted he ever saw her. To be seen was not her purpose, but to watch Oli operate in his natural habitat while not realizing he was being watched. He appeared to be consistent in his lunchtime habits, he always sat with the same two colleagues and he didn't act too flirty with the women he encountered. His manners were impeccable and these particular colleagues seemed to really like and enjoy his company. The cafeteria style eatery was huge, so remaining unseen was pretty easy for Mya, but she knew she had to be careful...the spy game could be tricky.

With that being said, on this day, she almost got caught in her espionage game. She hadn't been paying close enough attention when stepping in line and boom...there he was, standing right in front of her. She was shook, backing right into the person in line behind her. He was more good looking up close and personal! Just being in his presence made her a tad warm in all the right and wrong places. She closed her eyes, inhaled the scent of his cologne, and thanked God for the beautiful work of art this man was!

THE BOSS LADY

He didn't notice her immediately which riled Mya some, but when he did, he looked in her eyes, holding her captive without saying a single word. She forgot her decision to finally approach him as he proceeded through the line still as quiet as a church mouse. There was no need to say anything, Oli had her and he knew it. The future mother of his children, standing there like a vision, smooth as butter. Mya was so caught up, she didn't notice that Oli had paid for his lunch, as well as hers, and left the eatery. She had it bad.

"HELLO!!!" Mya snapped out of it when the cashier yelled at her to keep the line moving. How embarrassing.

"Oh, I'm so sorry," Mya states flustered. The cashier actually laughs.

"Honey, you need to move on out my line. You're so struck by that man, you didn't even notice he done paid for your lunch and gone on about his day. Everybody but you knows that man is wild about you. Girl, you better snatch that man up...him one of the good ones". With that, Mya stepped out of line, embarrassed and ready to get out of there.

When she got back to her office, still quite embarrassed yet a little giddy, she realized she wasn't hungry any longer. So, as she sat in her chair, watching the snow drift downward, she started to daydream..

She is on the beach with the sun kissing her body, when she feels the strongest hands touch her. These hands start to caress her while applying sunscreen. A massage of climactic proportions is what this is turning into, not that Mya is complaining. The hands, that have claimed her body, are moving with purpose and pleasure from her shoulders down the middle of her back, working out the kinks she didn't even know she had. As the magic hands knead her back like dough, Mya moans softly. There is extensive rubbing and caressing in a fashion that's making her warm and almost drunk with pleasure. The pivotal point of greatest satisfaction was within reach, but at that moment, she was startled back to reality by the ringing of the damn phone.

"Hello," she answered, a woman pissed off. Her attitude changed when she heard the voice of possibility on the other end.

"Hello sweetness", says Oli.

Chapter 16

<u>The Beat Goes On</u>

Eric decided the hell with it all, life goes on, right? No sign of Mya, who the hell knew where Angel was, and why should he care? He had a beautiful woman trying with all her might to get with him and he was pushing her off, why? That was what he was about to find out.

Mya knew she needed to come clean with Eric and tell him about Oli. But, exactly what would she be telling? That he piqued her curiosity? That she found him more interesting than Eric? That was all true, of course, but maybe it was just that Oli was "new". New in the sense that he was like a breath of fresh air on a very stale day. She didn't want to hurt Eric but there seemed to be no way around it.

THE BOSS LADY

The night Eric rushed to Mya's home, only to find her missing, hadn't turned out at all as either had expected. After that second bottle of wine and all those tears, Mya got a little bold; she called Oli. He came to her place, saw she was a wreck and decided the only thing he could do was take her to neutral ground...his house. In his haste to get Mya's purse and put her in the car, he just didn't close the door all the way, thus Eric finding the house with the door open when he arrived.

Upon arriving at Oli's, she was still a mess. He had the prize but, no matter the circumstances, he just couldn't take advantage of a woman in that state. He led her inside to his overstuffed couch, sitting with her as she continue to cry her eyes out. It wasn't until much later that she was able to tell him why she was crying. He didn't care, she was with him and that was all that mattered. They fell asleep on the couch, holding one another tightly. Mya slept like she hadn't in weeks. With Angel gone and Eric hurting her feelings, she felt as though she had taken a blow to the ribs. It was a lot to take in…things had been screwed every since Lincoln's death.

Mya woke up on a strange couch, not sure how she'd gotten there. She remembered the fight with Eric, the wine, and a phone call, but…*Oh hell! What have I done and with whom*, was her first troubled thought.

She stumbled from the couch, grabbed her aching head, and took a look see around the exquisite home. She marveled at the fine art work on the walls and mantel piece, still looking for some sign as to where she might be.

As she explored the massive living and dining quarters, she realized how beautiful and elegant this place really was. Her next thought made her nervous, *what if he shares this beautiful space with someone? Oh shit! Just because he never mentioned anyone, doesn't mean there was no one to mention.* Ugh…The memory of them sitting and talking into the wee hours slammed into her brain, just as that thought hit.

THE BOSS LADY

She smelled the most wonderful scent wafting from the kitchen, so she followed her nose. There she found the most wonderful array of pastries, fruits and flowers. There was Oli standing at the stove, whistling while he worked, looking comfortable and in his element. She just watched, as his body moved with ease, another fine work of art in a t-shirt and pajama pants. *Oh my*, she thought, *what am I going to do?*

As if he'd read her mind, Oli turned and said, "You are going upstairs to freshen up for breakfast." He put down the spatula, walked over to her and planted a juicy kiss right on her lips. It took her breath away. *What a greeting first thing in the morning? And, I haven't even brushed my teeth!* That was a major no-no for Eric; you had to apply some type of mouthwash before even looking in his direction.

Without hesitation and smiling like a school girl, she followed Oli up the ornate staircase. He led her into a bathroom almost as big as the entire upstairs of her house. There were Jack and Jill sinks with lights everywhere. The linens were almost too plush to touch. The toilet was in its own private space, with the shower separated from the massive Jacuzzi bathtub by a wall of thick, frosted glass blocks. Beautifully antiqued pictures and artwork gleamed on the walls surrounding the room. He then led her to a bedroom just through the opposite door, where she found toiletries and a change of clothes. They were not her personal things yet, they were new and they fit. It wasn't possible he had planned all this because he'd had no way of knowing she would call him the night before, but she had to hand it to him…he had made some serious moves with what little time he'd had. *This morning's breakfast is gonna be interesting indeed…*

———————————

Time waits for no man, you either keep up or get left behind. Eric didn't plan on getting left behind…again. It appeared Mya had done just that and he didn't like it at all. The message went something like this:

THE BOSS LADY

Hey Eric…I'm sorry you couldn't reach me last night, but after our conversation, I just needed some time to clear my head and do some thinking…I'm still clearing my head and thinking. Once I know my thoughts, I'll make sure to let you know them. I'll call you…bye. And that had said it all.

He knew there would be times when he'd wonder what he'd missed, what he hadn't done or could have done better, but those were all rhetorical questions now, that would never really be answered. On the upside, there was Autumn, who was soon to be his beautiful, smart, sexy ass new girlfriend. Mya who?

_____

Autumn was reaping the benefits of a boyfriend due to his issues with his prior girlfriend. He was all over her! Attentive, loving, compassionate, understanding, caring and a super listener. He was the complete package, right? Yeah…right!

BUSINESS LEFT UNFINISHED

Even though Autumn had gotten just what she wanted, she was ***not*** satisfied. She was selfish and she didn't like winning by default. She'd wanted to ***take*** him, not have him handed to her on a silver plated platter by his damn ex!

Despite their inner issues, they appeared to be a "happy" couple. They were certainly a most beautiful couple and Eric was definitely okay with their relationship. Autumn was having a bit more of a struggle. She liked the thrill of the chase and wasn't at all thrilled that ***her*** mission to seek and destroy had failed. She'd been hoping to annihilate Mya, for no other reason than it was what she wanted to do, just because she thought she could.

Business at the boutique had almost tripled due to a few cover stories on them as the city's new power couple. The designer suits Eric wore bore Autumn's signature and brought other men rushing into the shop to get the look. They were set apart from all the **Brooks Brothers** suits going up and down the street. Even new ladies were pouring in to find that perfect something for their man and themselves.

Eric, on the other hand, was basking in the fact that his new girlfriend was a great designer and he got to look so awesome for free. Problem was, he just didn't realize who his girlfriend *really* was and her MO.

Autumn was *already* looking for someone new. Even though her shop was doing well, she had done this song and dance before; about 5 times in the past 5 years. The outcome was usually the same. Whisk into town, set up shop, take some woman's man, gloat a bit, make tons of money then roll out. She had made herself a promise; the next man she took, she would work hard to maintain a reasonably healthy relationship with. She *did* like Eric more than the other losers she usually wound up with but all the real challenge had been taken out of it, and without the challenge, there was nothing to excite her.

BUSINESS LEFT UNFINISHED

Autumn had never had many friends…okay, she'd never had **any** real friends. She always alienated other females. Usually because she was always working on taking their boyfriends, or at least, having sex with them.

There was this one beautiful specimen of a caramel colored man named Terrance. Terrance had been the epitome of male loveliness. Oh the things Terrance did to her and oh how she enjoyed every stinking minute of it. She met Terrance, or rather his girlfriend Nyssa, by what appeared to be a total coincidence.

Autumn had been helping a "friend" set up a display in **her** mom's boutique, years ago, when in walked Terrance. Damn. Autumn had to catch her breath as she watched Nyssa smile while Terrance headed her way. Nyssa planted an obvious "we are more than just friends" kiss on him that made even Autumn blush. That was a big feat.

Terrance moved by Autumn, brushing her ever so slightly and she felt his warmth, smelled his scent and ogled his ass. She wanted that man, giving herself two weeks to accept and conquer the challenge. Every man she ever set her sights on required a time frame in which she gave herself to bed him; a little game she played. Evil and naughty, but she so enjoyed it.

Now her focus was always to go through the girlfriend, to make it seem like an innocent thing had gone oh so wrong, making the boyfriend the villain in the end. She didn't get Eric that way because Mya re-wrote the script. Although the outcome was the same, Autumn didn't like not controlling the situation. She was like a lioness in pursuit of the kill, once she set her mind to something and this time, she hadn't got the chance to bring her prey down her way. In her mind, she remembered what it had been like with Terrance. She had put in too much work for that tasty morsel and she was not conceding until she had blood on her jowls. Terrance's heart had beat a little too fast, too soon which got him in a position he wasn't at all sure he could get out of but by that point, Autumn had that crazed look in her eyes. She had gotten lost in the moment and Terrance had almost been in tears because he was actually scared his life was in grave danger.

Autumn shook the memory from her mind, reminding herself she was no longer a nineteen year old in High School. She now how bigger problems and bigger fish to fry. However, the inner pep talk didn't stop her from running her tongue over her lips to taste and enjoy the blood she found there. Caught in the thrill of the memory, she had damn near bitten a hole in her own lip...

Chapter 17

Eric

The day started in a rather peculiar fashion. Eric had agreed, against his penis' better judgment, to not spend the night with Autumn. Instead, he got up earlier and went to the boutique to do a little paperwork before heading into the office. He was working on a piece that could possibly win him a most coveted journalism award for the third time in a row.

Upon wrapping up his boutique business, the phone started ringing incessantly. He didn't answer it the first four times but by the fifth, he was a little miffed. The shop didn't open until 10 am, so who the hell would keep calling before nine?! He picked up and heard a commotion, like a riotous episode of the View. He was just about to hang up when he heard Autumn's name. Interest aroused, he listened closer, hearing such words as "hoax",

"Terrance", "sexual conquest" and "dirty whore", just to name a few. Eric, being the urban sophisticate he thought himself to be, was a little taken aback by the conversation, but curiosity wouldn't let him hang up or interrupt.

As the conversation continued, he learned more about Autumn's past than he could have heard from her parents…yeah, it got just that deep. He never would have imagined her being responsible for the kinds of nasty things he was hearing from the other end of the phone. *This has to be some type of set up or something by people who hate Autumn*, he tried to reason with himself. Yet, even as he thought it, the journalist in him said *there is truth in the story*. It wasn't until he heard **his** name and how she was planning to take out Mya that it all became too real.

Chapter 18

<u>Say Yes</u>

Angel and Sterling were living the life; loving each other like love is supposed to be. Mostly up, rarely down, there were a few times when the memory of Lincoln's death overcame her and she got a little edgy but Sterling went out of his way to help ease that pain. They even discussed having children from time to time but collectively decided that, although they had all this love to share, they wanted to be selfish and keep it to themselves...at least for the time being.

He decided it was pass the time to make Angel an honest woman. Although living together in sin was quite enjoyable, he wanted a wife, not just a live-in girlfriend. She was his help meet, his dream sharer and most definitely his best friend, so the next logical move was to make her his wife. There may be some challenge involved; Angel's best friend Mya wasn't too pleased with either of them right now. Angel had assured him she'd be able to smooth her girl's ruffled feathers when the time came.

According to Angel, she had just taken off without a word to anyone…not her sister, Mya, or any of the people associated with the daycare center. She'd just hopped in her car and drove. That had been several weeks ago and in all that time, she had only sent two half-assed messages to both Mya and her sister Felice. The first, telling them both that all was well and the second, simply letting them know she was in Wisconsin taking a much needed break. That was it! Neither of them knew anything about her being with him and that didn't sit well with Sterling. He didn't have much family, being kinda distant from what little he did have since his mother's death, so whenever he got the chance to get with his people, he jumped on it. He urged Angel, almost daily, to get in contact with her people and mend those fences but she was hesitant. Probably because she felt somewhat guilty for how she'd treated them when they'd only been trying to help her as best they knew how. However, now that he had marriage on his mind, it was something that needed to be handled sooner rather than later. He would approach her again this evening and make sure she finally did what she needed to do.

"Okay, okay…damn, I'll do it. I'll call them both. Will that make you happy?" Angel was heated but she knew Sterling was right. It was time for her to make real peace with her past and reach out to her loved ones. If she was honest, she'd admit she was scared of their reaction. She'd been wrong to just run off without a word to anyone and have everybody all worried about her. She'd left her sister to try to run the daycare center alone and God only knew how they were feeling about her right about now.

"Listen baby, I'm not tryna piss you off or upset you, I just want you to be happy and I know you miss your sister and yo girl. I see the way you look at the kids in the neighborhood…I know you miss the daycare kids too…" She really did miss them all and she missed her home. It was time to make it right.

Mya didn't answer, so Angel left her a detailed message, asking that she please return the call. Felice, on the other hand, answered before the second ring and their reunion was surprising as well as very touching.

"Hey Sis…uhm…I just…" Felice interrupted her immediately.

"Babygirl, are you okay? Where are you? What in the world are you doing in Wisconsin? You need to come home now Angel! We miss you and are all so very worried about you! What were you thinking to just run off like that girl? The kids haven't been the same since you disappeared…"

Tears of relief flooded her eyes as she relaxed in the embrace of her older sister's love and concern. It was gonna be alright with Felice.

THE BOSS LADY

"Have you got a couple of hours Sis? I got a story to tell and it's gonna take a minute…" They talked for hours, carefully avoiding too much talk about the past and the situation with Lincoln. This was a time for fresh, new starts and Felice was really anxious to meet Sterling. Her baby sister sounded happy, healthy, mentally stable, and if he was in any way responsible for that, she would welcome him with open arms. God had certainly heard and answered her prayers.

Dare we say, Mya was a different story. Don't misunderstand, she was thrilled and sooo relieved to hear from her friend, she just wasn't quite as gracious and willing to forgive Angel's behavior as Felice had been. As soon as she heard Angel's voice on the phone, her anger spiked and she went in…

"So trick, while we all here worried sick about yo ass, you somewhere half way across the planet laid up with some new nicca! What kinda f'd up shit is that Angel? If you just wanted to go out and find you some new meat, you coulda just said so instead of putting us through all this bullshit..."

Angel was hot-tempered as well, ready to strike back, but Sterling quietly reminded her Mya loved her and was just angry over how she'd handled the situation, with every right to be. Angel took a deep breath to release *her* rising anger and spoke quickly to shut her girl up.

"Mya boo, you are exactly right and I am so sorry for how I treated you. I handled the situation all wrong..." Mya was immediately rendered speechless. Never in all the years she'd known Angel, had she experienced her conceding that quickly. Girlfriend would put up a fight where there was no fight!

She continues, "...I had never gone through anything like that before, nothing even close and I didn't know what the hell I was supposed to do with all the feelings, the guilt, but that didn't give me the right to mistreat the people that I love and love me. I had to get away from it all Mya or I was gonna go crazy, but I should have told you guys my plans so you wouldn't be so worried. I'm in a much, much better place now, mentally and emotionally, and I'm praying you'll find it in your heart to forgive me for just being human and acting on impulse…"

It's was around 4 am when Angel finally cuddled next to her man, tired, yet truly happy and at peace for the first time in many months. He'd been right, making peace with her past and her people was what she'd really needed.

Before she closed her eyes to drift into restful sleep, she saw Lincoln but this time there was no gaping wound, no haunted eyes and no blood. His face bore the most serene smile, his eyes twinkled and peace seemed to envelope him like a blanket.

As his image faded, she silently thanked heaven for her life, her health, her family and most importantly, her love.

———————————————

BUSINESS LEFT UNFINISHED

With all finally well on the home front, Sterling set out to plan the most romantic proposal he could muster. Mya and Felice helped him pick out the ring, as they both knew what Angel would love, and being women, they could give him pointers on how to make it truly special. It was a gorgeous, high standing princess cut solitaire with diamond baguettes all around the thick band. Sterling decided to take her to the Eagle's Nest for the most memorable dinner, in full dress as he asked for her hand in marriage.

It was a beautiful summer evening. The sky was clear and the sun was setting. The dusk sky, arrayed in so many amazing colors, offered the perfect backdrop. He arranged for them to eat on the balcony, making all the staff on duty aware of what was happening. Angel wore the most beautiful summer dress; a soft, blush chiffon that hung loose to her heel encased feet but clung to her every curve when she moved. It was sheer, without being too revealing and the color made her dark chocolate skin pop. She had no idea this was a proposal dinner; she'd been told they were meeting a few of his business associates for a night out. So Angel was a bit surprised when she saw the balcony table set for a romantic dinner for two but didn't give it a lot of thought. When the lanterns were lit, the champagne brought out and the soft sound of Tamia and Eric Bonet singing "**Spend My Life With You**" settled on her ears, she knew something more than a night out was at hand. That was *their* song, so Angel began to sing along.

As she sang, Sterling motioned for the maître'd to bring over the dozen long stem white roses hidden under a silver dome…she squealed in delight. These were her favorite flower and as she investigated, she noticed something gleaming in the petals of one rose. The ring had been strategically tucked into the soft whiteness, almost invisible except for the high shine. Just as realization dawned on her, Sterling went on one knee, taking her hands into his.

"My Angel, my love, my friend…I ask you on this day to take my hand and be my wife. I can't imagine my life without you and I don't want to waste anymore time in changing your last name to mine. Will you be my wife?" Tears flowed freely from her eyes, as well as his, while the entire restaurant waited with bated breath for her answer.

"Yes…" it came out as just above a whisper. Sterling wasn't sure he'd heard her until she spoke it again "…yes, I will gladly be your wife…" The crowd erupted in applause and whoops of congratulations!

Chapter 19

<u>Welcome Back</u>

The breakfast had been awesome and the company even better, yet, it had been a struggle for Mya. Oli was one good looking man, she was one confused woman, and sometimes that didn't make for such a good combination. Thankfully, Oli wasn't the type to take advantage of a situation just because there was a situation. Yeah, he wanted her badly, but she had to come to him willingly, not because she was messed up over some other dude. He wasn't just some guy you picked up on the rebound.

With that being said, he fed her, dressed her, comforted her, then securely planted her right back at her place without being touched. If a man can't control his hormones, he was no real man!

BUSINESS LEFT UNFINISHED

"I enjoyed your company and thank you for everything. You have been the perfect gentleman and I appreciate that…" She *did* appreciate it but he could have tried a lil something something.

"You needed a friend, you reached out and I answered your need. Look Mya, I don't think there's any misunderstanding here. You know how I feel and I know you do. I know how *you* feel, even if you're not sure. I'll be here when you are sure…just please don't take too long…"

Now he was on the phone, dripping with charm and making her drip in secret places…

"Hello sweetness…" he said, she smiled.

"So, I gather you have known for a minute that I've been stalking you at lunch. Why didn't you say anything?"

He laughed, "At first I was a bit pissed off, then I realized it was your way of getting to know me without getting to know me. You women are strange creatures, with strange habits but who can live without you? So I'll let you play your little game until you decide to get tired. Just don't play too long sweetness, cause I don't much like games." She understood perfectly.

"Neither do I Oli, and I apologize. It didn't start out as a game. It was just easier to watch silently than to approach you. Despite my obvious bossiness, I can be real shy sometimes. Plus, after our little bus incident, I was trying to convince myself that I don't much like you…" They both broke into laughter, relaxing the atmosphere 100%.

"Well, since I paid for your lunch, I guess I have no choice but to buy your dinner as well; especially considering you turned me down the first time I asked you out."

From that moment on, at least for the next several weeks, they were inseparable. They placed no label on their relationship, just wanting it to have the freedom to go where it was meant to go. It was fresh, fun and without demands…they were taking the time to really get to know one another and even learn some new things about themselves.

During this time, Mya was reconciled with Angel, learning she was about to get engaged to Sterling. She also learned that Eric had started dating this other young lady. Autumn Matthews was a business owner/designer and after seeing her in some local newspaper article, Mya thought she looked vaguely familiar. She wasn't sure how she felt about this newest development; however, she and Oli were having so much fun, she didn't give it a lot of thought. She, Angel and Felice were planning a wedding, life was good; she intended to allow nothing to bring her down. Then she got a call from Eric that shook her to the core...

Chapter 20

<u>Never Saw This Coming</u>

So this little bitch thinks she's slick, Eric reasoned, as he processed the info he'd stumbled upon in that conversation he was sure he wasn't supposed to hear. As articulate and educated as Eric prided himself on being, he was from the hood. The hood had raised him, taught him the skills that made him an award-winning reporter, and was now showing him how to handle little Miss Autumn. She'd had the audacity to come to his city and try to play a player…he would show her ass a thing or two about the game. Maybe this dude Terrance hadn't known how to work her, but he was Eric "the snake" McGhee…the snake was real, smooth, and always struck his prey so fast they didn't know what hit em.

A plan was formulating in his head, *this little trick had messed with the right one this time*, the snake hissed. He would have to contact Mya, letting her know she needed to pay attention to her surroundings because this crazy bitch was out to get her. It was one thing to come for him, but together or not, Mya was off limits…point, blank, PERIOD!

Eric checked the caller id to see if the number had been recorded…it was listed as private, but he had a friend that could decode anything. He would start there…finding out where and possibly whom that call had come from. The reporter in him wanted to know more about this Terrance dude. Who was he and exactly how was he connected to Autumn and her sorted past?

Much to his relief, he found that voicemail had actually recorded the entire conversation, giving him the opportunity to listen to it as many times as needed so he could pull all the info he wanted from it. He played it over and over, speeding it up then slowing it down. His instincts telling him which clues to listen for; sounds, background noises, other conversations that may have been happening simultaneously. His story for the paper was set aside for now; this was much more important.

Now Eric understood why Autumn would never talk about her family or her past. He'd tried on several occasions to get her to open up but she'd always used sex as a way to change the subject. I mean sure, they had nasty, mind blowing sex. Who knew a sex swing could do so much? The things she could do with her tongue almost made him forget his name.

However, despite the intensity of those sessions, Eric knew there had to be more than sex to manage a halfway decent relationship. He wanted to get to the core of who Autumn was. Why did she not want him to tap into her past? What was she hiding? Those were his thoughts then, but she'd made him completely forget them with her sexual antics…now he saw the big picture and it was ugly as hell!

Locked in the editing office at the newspaper, he typed in her name and birth date on Google, just to see what surfaced. It took a few searches and he had to narrow it down a few times, but, what he came up with both shocked and didn't shock him at the same time. There were stories about drugs with mugshots, schemes, scams and some real shady shit. The name Terrance came up again in connection to her, so Eric decided he would start there. He just hoped this Terrance dude was mad enough at Autumn to help him finally put an end to her criminal bullshit...

———————————

Terrance was stuck. He couldn't help but allow his mind to wander back to her. He'd never considered himself a player, always priding himself on being faithful to whomever he was seeing. Autumn had played him like a drum and he still didn't like it. He wanted revenge because he'd lost a great deal due to her games. For him, Nyssa would forever be the one that got away when she was the one he wanted most to stay. That bitch Autumn owed him!

After the situation at the shop, Terrance allowed himself to be taken advantage of by Autumn. He found himself lured into her trap over and over again. She'd set his ass up something awful. He'd been so caught up, he'd found himself blatantly flirting with and getting real cozy with Autumn during those double dates she always managed to arrange but somehow never had a date for. Nyssa was beginning to call Autumn out on this and somehow Autumn turned the tables on Nyssa, accusing her of being a horrible friend, and putting poor Terrance in the middle. The last straw for Nyssa was unfortunate but Autumn had set it up just right. Another couples night...

Terrance had gotten there early, since he came right from work and conveniently, Autumn had some items she needed some muscle for...Terrance was that muscle.

BUSINESS LEFT UNFINISHED

Autumn wanted to make sure when Nyssa walked in, there would be no doubt that he was either sexing Autumn or wanted to really badly. In true Autumn Matthew's form, she'd made things look as bad as they possibly could, even under the best of circumstances.

With Terrance on a ladder and oblivious to her plan, she strategically placed herself in front of him and eye level with his penis. As she instructed him on what she wanted where, keeping him preoccupied, she eased his zipper down. Before he knew what was happening, his penis was in her hand, just as Nyssa walked in. It was a hot ass mess after that. Nyssa was done and Terrance was stunned, with his denials and explanations falling on deaf ears. Autumn had even managed to somehow involve him in some drug-related shit she had going on at the time. It had taken many months and not a few thousands of dollars for his parents to finally clear his name.

Oh yeah, he was definitely ready to see this bitch fry for all she had cost him. *Maybe I should connect with this Eric McGhee dude and let him know what a real snake he's messing with,* Terrance considered, as he slammed the newspaper on the table.

"Look, even though things didn't work out with us, I had to call and let you know what this bitch is up to so you can be prepared. It appears she's involved in a lot of shady shit, but I got all that covered. I just need you to stay on your toes until I can get this handled…"

Under any other circumstances, Eric might have felt some type of way just calling her out of the blue, but this was some different level shit and he wasn't the Eric she knew; he was the old Eric, before writing and reporting changed his life. It was a shame this mess had him reverting back to old ways, but the shame was on Autumn.

"...I'm sending a pic of her to your phone as we speak. I don't know if you've ever seen her but it's obvious she knows you. Just be real careful and real smart Mya, at least until I let you know all is well."

Mya was speechless for a moment. Why would this chick still be after her, when she posed no threat to whatever relationship she had with Eric? Some 21st century women, with all the progress that had been made, could still be real stupid when it came to men…she just didn't get it. Her phone beeped to notify her of the incoming text and she looked deep in Autumn Matthews eyes. Yes, it was the same woman she'd seen in the newspaper article and the cover of **UPTOWN MAGAZINE**; it was also the same woman she had seen in a couple of her dreams. What the hell was really going on?!She was a gorgeous woman; you couldn't look at her and tell she apparently had some serious social and mental issues.

"Mya…are you there?" The sound of his voice brought her out of her musings.

"Uhm…yeah, I'm still here…this just really makes no kind of sense to me. I've seen her before in the newspaper and magazine…" she chose to keep the dreams to herself "…why would she come for me when she has you? I don't get it but then, I don't get a lot of shit nowadays."

Eric just shook his head, "I have no idea. Based on what I've learned of her past, coming after the girlfriend or ex is part of her MO. Believe me when I tell you, this one is a real piece of work. *YOU* just keep your eyes and ears open and I'll give you the head's up when the coast is clear…"

Mya didn't like the way Eric was talking; he sounded nothing like himself, but then, this wasn't your every day, run of the mill situation. She knew he was up to something, that much was clear and to be quite honest, she didn't want to know what it was.

"Thanks Eric, I really appreciate you contacting me…uhm…*you* be careful and watch your back. Sounds like this one knows a few things about underhanded shit so don't underestimate her. Keep me posted please." He promised to contact her as soon as everything was Gucci, told her to take care and was gone.

Mya sat at her desk just looking at the picture of Autumn, wondering how Eric had got them in this mess. Men needed to learn that every pretty face and fat ass didn't bring a pretty mind with it. She was sure his penis was to blame but…maybe this woman was just crazy period. It would definitely make for some interesting conversation tonight over dinner with Oli and she couldn't wait to call Angel to fill her in. Damn!

Chapter 21

<u>The Boys Are Back In Town</u>

Eric made a few more calls, reaching all the wrong people named Terrance; one had actually been a female with the deepest, sexiest voice. *You ain't got time for that shit man*, he scolded himself and pressed on. He had two numbers left on his list and disappointment was setting in. He hoped he wouldn't have to use his other sources but he would if push came to shove.

He dialed, the phone rang, voicemail. Feeling the old surge of anger rising in him, he called the last number... it rang, a dude answered.

"Who the fuck is dis?!" This dude sounded pissed!

"Uhm...hello...may I speak with Terrance?"

"Who wants him?" The dude's attitude was starting to piss *him* off. He remained calm. If this was the Terrance he was looking for, he needed the dude to keep being pissed.

"My name is Eric McGhee and I'm calling in regards to what I hope is a mutual friend. A woman known as Autumn Matthews. Would you happen to know her?"

Terrance smiled. *Looks like the powers that be have saved me the trouble of making a call*! Yet, he proceeded with some caution. With that bitch, you just never knew.

"And what if I do? What is it to you?"

"Well, if this is Terrance Blanch, I would assume your family spent a lot of money getting you outta all the shit that piece got you into for nothing and I was hoping we might be able to work out a little something special for Miss Matthews…"

THE BOSS LADY

"So, the bitch burned you too huh?" Terrance didn't miss a beat, "...sign me up for that homie. That bitch damn near ruined my life. I'm still mad and she don't even give a fuck. I see she's still going around screwing with people. Yeah, I definitely think it's time for her to be taught a real valuable lesson. So, what you thinking partner? How you plan on bringing the bitch down". Eric just sat there smiling at this dude's willingness to clap back on this bitch. She must have hurt him real bad.

"Yeah bruh, I'm among the burnt and sizzling. The bitch thinks she's slick and I hate a slick bitch. If you're gonna be rude and nasty as hell, just be rude and nasty as hell...don't fake the funk. She thinks she owns the game, but I wanna teach her how to really play...feel me my dude?" He had to shake himself; he was getting a little too comfortable in his old skin.

"Hell yeah, I feel ya man. I've been waiting for the opportunity to nail that hoe for over ten years. Woulda been done it but I had to watch my steps cause the Feds was watching em too. Do yo have any idea what it's like to be on the government's radar and you ain't even done shit?! That shit is crazy!"

Eric wanted to keep Terrance talking; the more he talked, the angrier he became and his anger was essential to Eric's plan.

"Yeah man, I was reading a lil bit about what happened but it didn't make much sense to me..."

Terrance then explains to Eric how the whole sorry episode had gone down. What he hadn't known was, the shit he'd been moving and stacking on the shelf that day, while she had his penis in her hand, was **Class A** Colombian smack. The shit they was killing for all over the country and there he was all up in it, with his young, dumb ass.

When the bust had finally gone down, Autumn named Terrance as the middle man for the supplier. The bitch lied through her pretty little teeth! And, with his fingerprints all over the damn boxes, he was left holding the proverbial bag. If it hadn't been for his parents having the means to afford him a damn good attorney and the surveillance tapes proving Terrance hadn't been a part of any of the other deals and shipments, he would probably still be locked up in some Federal prison somewhere.

The Feds weren't stupid either, and it didn't take them long to realize Terrance was just a sprung teenager being set up, but the D.A. was trying to get re-elected and used the case to take a stand on drugs. Terrance was still paying his peeps back...it had cost them pretty penny. Whether or not he was still on the radar, remained to be seen, but Terrance never went a day without feeling like he was being watched. So yeah, he had an ax to grind. It was the principal of the thing, at this point. Eric felt bad for the brother. To have to deal with some shit like that, having done nothing, must have been rough.

They agreed to meet in person; talking over the phone was too risky for what Eric had in mind. It was time to hit back and they was finna hit back hard. *Watch out Autumn, your season is just about up.*

Eric decided to meet in a place where folks met up to handle the type of business they needed to handle; Joe's Pool Hall. Joe was the meanest muthafucka in town, although most people didn't know that, including Joe. He was ex-military, with skills beyond belief. He was also cool with the less desirable members of society and for that reason, he was pleasantly known as the Ghetto Jesus. What went on at Joe's stayed at Joe's cause it was rumored that the few people that had left running their mouths, were never seen or heard from again. Everybody's business wasn't everybody's business, at least that was Joe's take on it.

Terrance arrived first, took a booth in the back and order a drink. Eric arrived soon after, slid into the massive booth across from Terrance and order a drink as well. As luck would have it, due to the growing demand for her designs, Autumn needed to open a larger store. She was in the process of looking for a much larger space, with Eric's help of course. With the right amount of cash, the perfect set up was easily arranged. Four men with two trucks were hired for this job. One truck to move Autumn into her roomy new space, the other to move all the extras in right along side those brand new designer pieces. The drugs, the guns, and other illegal contraband were all easily acquired at their one stop shopping spot, Joe's Pool Hall.

Chapter 22

<u>Down She Goes</u>

Autumn was clueless, exactly the way Eric intended to keep her. Ever since the morning he'd heard that ominous conversation, he'd been overly attentive and loving with her. He was so sickeningly sweet, he almost made himself wanna puke! However, in order for his plan to work, he had to keep her convinced she was still in control and running the show. The bitch was an egotistical maniac, a psychopath that had to be monitored at all times.

She was also a nympho, sex being her drug of choice and Eric had no problem giving her fix after fix after fix. He had to add a few supplements to his daily routine just to keep up with her. Luckily, the growing business, the anticipation of moving into a larger shop, and the sex kept her so preoccupied, he could continue his plans without her suspecting a thing. He'd even manufactured a scene where he ripped into "Mya" over the phone, in Autumn's hearing, telling her to leave him alone...that it was over between them and he had found a much better woman in Autumn. This finally brought her some of the satisfaction she'd been seeking in the beginning. It wasn't quite the same as *her* destroying Mya, yet the sound of her pleading with him then breaking out in heart wrenching sobs just before he hung up on her, made Autumn's heart beat just a bit faster and got Eric a lap dance that was to die for. He was well rewarded for that performance. Little did she know, it was just one of his co-workers on the other line...she too was well rewarded for her performance.

Since things were going so well with the business, simply meaning she was securing great bags, Eric was being such a good boy and her competition had been brought to her knees, Autumn decided she would stay in town a bit longer. She would ride this gravy train until at least one wheel popped off.

After the drug bust and the '*too close for comfort*' escape from her last scheme, she'd prided herself on not staying anywhere too long. Greed and feelings would get you into a lot of trouble if you weren't careful and trouble was not something she wanted. She wanted money, excitement, power and sex...all the nasty, hot sex she could get, and for now, Eric was giving her all that and more.

Two more magazine articles and another newspaper article, had Autumn feeling like she owned the city and she **could** do much worse than having one of the most sought after bachelors in town as her man. He, the award-winning journalist on the rise; she, the hottest new designer/ entrepreneur in town...they were truly the Dynamic Duo.

One afternoon, about two weeks after Eric had learned her secret, she walked into his office wearing nothing but a men's trench coat, red-bottom stilettos and a smile. She had locked his door, dropped the coat and fucked the hell outta him right there on his desk. For a split second, he questioned his decision to do this bitch in, but he knew she couldn't be trusted and he was already tired of sleeping with one eye open.

"Baby…" she purrs from her laid back position on his office sofa "…don't be too upset, but I've arranged for us to take a mini vacay a few days before we move into the new shop. We could use some time off and once we get settled, there won't be any time for play." He panicked but maintained his outward composure. Everything was in place…going away would fuck up the plan.

"Babe, are you sure? I thought you'd want to spend that time advertising and building anticipation for the grand opening. Are you sure that would be a good time to go away and be outta the public view? Don't you have a couple of interviews and a photo shoot around that time?" He would have to find a way to make sure this mini vacay shit never happened.

"Yes, I did but I canceled all that. I'm tired and I want to go away for a few days…somewhere exotic and sexy, where I can have sex on the beach all day if I want."

Eric knew better than to try to change her mind once it was set on something. There was no reasoning with her when she was having one of her "spoiled little girl" moments. So, he conceded, determined to figure out how to keep them in town, right where they needed to be.

With all that was going on, Mya was glad for her relationship with Oli and Angel's wedding preparations. It helped to keep her grounded and thinking about positive things. She'd received another message from Eric, telling her she could relax some but not to become careless. As far as he was concerned, the threat still remained. He assured her the threat would be totally removed in the next couple of weeks.

Oli had been just as dumbfounded as she; why would this woman still be coming after Mya when she had the man? He was even more cautious than she was, almost not letting her out of his sight the first few days after she told him.

Angel, on the other hand, hadn't been surprised at all. She'd always said women were crazy as bedbugs when it came to men, hence the reason she only dealt with Mya, her sister and a few family members. She had a few female associates, but Angel had always dealt better with men as friends. She'd also been ready to hop on the first plan to deal with Autumn herself. It had taken some serious talking on the part of Mya and Sterling to change her mind.

BUSINESS LEFT UNFINISHED

"I'm taking the first flight out in the morning. Bitch wanna play, I'll show her how to play..." That was Angel, quiet, subdued and always ready to open a can of kick ass when needed.

Now Mya and Oli were on a flight headed to Wisconsin to spend the weekend with the future Mr. & Mrs. Sterling Larson. They both needed a break, plus, they had fittings for wedding dresses. Felice was also due to arrive sometime over the weekend. Her husband had agreed to stay home with their children so she could have some much needed "me" time. It would be great to finally meet Sterling and just get together to chill.

They were met at the train station by Sterling; Angel was in real estate class. She'd always desired to be a real estate agent and Sterling had convinced her to take the online class in her spare time. Mya had seen Sterling once or twice at his mom's house but they'd never met. She liked him immediately, although she couldn't have told you why exactly. There was just something very pleasant and calming about his aura; something that made you think of lightness and peace in his presence. She could tell that Oli felt it as well.

She embraced him, totally comfortable with him and spoke with an easy smile, "Glad to finally meet the man making Angel an honest woman. I'm Mya and this is Oli…" His smile was bright and genuine, causing his eyes to twinkle like a mischievous boy.

He gave Oli some dap, looking him straight in the eye, then responded to her, "well, hello there Mya and Oli. Good to finally meet you both. Now let's go get this reunion started right!"

There was no awkward silence or dead air during the ride to their hotel, then to Oli's. The conversation flowed easily between the three of them. It was as though they'd known one another for years.

If Mya liked Sterling before, she loved him once she saw her best friend. Angel was glowing and looking better than Mya had ever seen her. She'd lost a few pounds, toned up in a few places, and cut her hair in a new style that framed her face beautifully, accentuating those big, lovely eyes. She looked great physically; however, the beauty was not coming from the outward but the inward. This woman was glowing from the inside out!

Mya experienced that same sense of peace and calm radiating from Angel, just as it radiated from Sterling. It was obvious this man was good for her in every way. She looked happy, healthy but most of all, loved.

"Biotch, I oughta whoop dat ass for all the worry you caused me, but damn, it's good to see you Sis! And a bitch looking tight too…" Angel laughed, throwing herself into her best friend's arms. It was at that moment that she realized just how much she'd missed her girl!

"Heifer, I have missed you and all that damn mouth!" This was the beginning of a girl to girl session that lasted into the wee hours of the morning. Acknowledging their need to reconnect, Oli and Sterling left them alone for the next several hours. It was basketball season, both men were huge NBA fans, so they found plenty to occupy their time.

They talked about everything, from playground to bedroom. Angel was finally able to talk about Lincoln and what had happened, without guilt or any sense of shame.

"I *know* I handled *that* all wrong but girl, I just felt so guilty and lost. I kept making myself somehow responsible for what he did and it took a *whole* minute for me to accept that it had been his decision. It really had nothing to do with me. If he'd been with another woman, he would have done the same thing. It was a burden to bare, let me tell you, and if it had not been for God reminding me of Sterling's letter, I honestly don't know where I'd be right now. I want to apologize to you again Sis, for my behavior but girl…that shit was rough!"

Mya took her hand, "No need for anymore apologies. I can't begin to imagine what that must have been like for you and I'm sorry I wasn't more patient and helpful. As your friend, I wanted to be there for you but I just didn't know how, so I pushed…pushing way too hard."

"You did help, I just had to find myself again. Thank goodness I was already on the road to recovery when I picked up the phone to reach out to Sterling. He really has changed my life, you know. I can't wait to be his wife and maybe have a baby or two…and, can I just say you and Oli look good together. You look happy. I like him."

THE BOSS LADY

The mention of Oli brought a huge smile to Mya's face, "We're taking it slow Sis, adding no labels. Just enjoying life and each other...yeah...I'm happy and there is no doubt Sterling is the man for you. He got a thot looking like a wife..." They broke into peals of laughter. They weren't even tired the next morning, although Mya and Oli had to rush back to the hotel to shower and change.

Felice came in on the noonday train. They scooped her up, heading straight for the bridal shop. The dresses were coming along nicely, with a tuck here and a nip there. Had it been left up to Angel, she would have gladly married Sterling at the courthouse; he wasn't having it. He wanted a wedding with all the trimmings. His mom had always expressed her dismay at never having a wedding, so this was also his way of honoring her. Angel would have the finest wedding he could provide and he would live his mother's unrealized dream.

BUSINESS LEFT UNFINISHED

Upon leaving the shop, the three ladies sat for a late lunch at Empire Restaurant, enjoying the fine red wine they offered and one another's company. They messed around and got tipsy, ending up in Mya's hotel room, with more wine, talking and laughter.

"I clearly remember my wedding night..." Felice replied, sipping her wine, "...he was more nervous than me. Dude sprayed everywhere in less than five minutes. I was so pissed, I thought about having the damn thing annulled. Thank God the nicca finally got it right!!!" Mya laughed so hard, she spewed wine all over everybody, which made them laugh even harder.

"Sterling is an excellent lover, so he already know he bet not eff up my wedding night. I will beat his ass if he taps out on me!" Angel had that "I mean that shit" look on her face and it was hilarious.

THE BOSS LADY

Four hours later, Sterling and Oli found them passed out in the hotel room, several empty wine bottles littered the floor around them. *Strange creatures*, Oli thought to himself as he helped Mya sober up a bit, *with strange habits, but who can live without them*?

The weekend had been a huge success! Mending fences, re-establishing relationships and starting new ones. The next time they all came together, it would be at Angel and Sterling's wedding, just a few weeks away. The two fellas had also done a lot of talking and Oli was ready. He planned to propose to Mya as soon as they got back home. No point in wasting anymore time…he knew he had found his Ms. Right.

How did Eric stop the vacay plans? Easily. He drugged the bitch, causing them to miss their flight to

Jamaica. The solution to the problem had some to him purely by chance…or, was it?

A couple of days after their conversation, Autumn had come down with a terrible sinus infection, yet, she was still determined to get away. Her doctor had prescribed some powerful antibiotics, as well as some pain medication. Eric took this unforeseen turn of events to kill any possibility of them leaving town.

The night before they were scheduled to leave, he upped the dosage of her pain medication, causing her to sleep for a solid 14 hours. She woke up groggy, disoriented and ready for more sleep, so, he gave her a sedative. By the time she woke again, another 10 hours later, the flight had been missed and the opportunity gone.

Autumn was pissed but she couldn't blame anyone else and she wasn't into taking responsibility for anything. So, in true Autumn Matthews style, she said nothing about missing the vacay, since it was on her, and kept her money train moving right along. Had Eric been the one to get sick, all hell would have broken loose.

Eric breathed a silent sigh of relief, knowing his plans for her would go uninterrupted and soon he could reveal how he truly felt about her. The mere thought of what was about to happen, made him giddy. He was intoxicated with the notion of giving this bitch just what she deserved. He and Terrance had communicated one last time before the rendezvous at her new spot; they couldn't afford to be linked together in any way until this business was done and settled for good.

He woke with Autumn busy between his legs, giving him the wake up of all wake up calls. He was certainly gonna miss her sexual prowess...if only this mouth and body were attached to a woman with some morals that could be trusted. However, since she was doing her thing so well this morning, he wasn't complaining. He gladly joined in with the festivities. She freaked him in ways she'd never done before, almost as if she knew this would be one of their last encounters. It was damn near 11 am when they finally climbed out of bed to hit the shower. Once there, she worked him over again, so much so, his legs were almost too weak to hold him.

The truck arrived on schedule to pick up the last load to be moved; the second truck was around the corner from the new spot, waiting. When everything was placed in the shop, Autumn directed the movers as to where she wanted each piece specifically, so they went to work. She left, returning to the old building to make sure nothing had been forgotten. While she was gone, the second truck was unloaded, with enough illegal drugs, guns and other contraband strategically placed among the furnishings, bolts of material, racks of designs being positioned in the space. They followed her instructions meticulously, making sure she would have no reason to delve too deeply or move things around too much.

This moving and placing continued until about 10 pm that night...the following morning was the grand opening and everything had to be perfect. Eric stayed with her throughout the day and night, assisting her in any way she needed him; secretly keeping his eyes on the various packages, bundles, and boxes containing his weapons against her. If she came too close to anything, he'd pop up to take on that chore so she could do something else.

The whole operation almost crashed when she discovered one of his packages among her display of newly designed scarves. He just happened to walk back in as she was about to unwrap it. He was tempted to snatch it out of her hand but that would make her hella suspicious, so he called her name in an excited voice, startling her and causing her to drop the package.

"Autumn! Look what I found in the back of the truck!" She wheeled around to blast his ass for scaring the shit out of her, then smiled like an angel when she glimpsed what was in his hand.

"Oh my goodness, you found my bracelet! I thought I'd lost it for sure. Why in the world was it in the truck?" Package forgotten, she reached for the diamond encrusted tennis bracelet. It was the only thing she had to remember her mother and it was priceless to her. Eric had taken it just in case he could use it in his plan…good thing he'd been thinking ahead.

"Hell, I don't know. Maybe it came off in one of the sofas in the old shop and got dropped while the guys were moving the furniture. I'm just glad I found it. You really seemed bummed about losing it…" He let a little concern lace his words.

"Oh yes, it's very precious to me for several reasons. Thank you so much. You deserve something special for this…" Eric knew that look and so did his penis. He was hard as a brick before she even touched him. He would have to try to remember to get that package back tucked in its spot before she thought about it again. But, for now, he was gonna enjoy the hands and hot, wet lips gliding over his sex fevered body.

The combination of bracelet and sex had worked perfectly. The heroine was back safely in its spot and they were back in bed celebrating their newest victory the way they loved to celebrate.

The morning of the GRAND OPENING dawned bright and sunny, with Autumn and Eric engaging in their usual breakfast for two, trying to take several bites out of each other.

BUSINESS LEFT UNFINISHED

The ribbon cutting was small and intimate, with only important people in the business, media, fashion and government arenas being invited. However, someone had made a call to local law enforcement about the drugs and guns stashed in the shop and, much to Autumn's surprise and dismay, these uninvited guest couldn't be forced to leave. They informed her of the allegations, produced the necessary search warrants, then went in with the dogs.

Sure as grits is groceries, they found all kinds of stuff. Guns, drugs, stolen jewelry and a huge amount of cash. It was like something out of a movie. It was also broadcast on every local news channel, with Autumn's face plastered all over the screen. The plan had been beautifully orchestrated and executed to a tee.

Eric played the shocked and humiliated boyfriend, as more and more detail from Autumn's past surfaced with each new report. Connecting her to the drugs and guns wouldn't be too hard, considering her past crimes and the fact that the shop was in her name alone. No one else's fingerprints were found on any of the illegal packages and boxes, and the Feds were all too happy to finally have enough evidence to deal with her appropriately. She wouldn't slip through their fingers this time by incriminating someone else.

Terrance and Eric enjoyed celebration shots at Joe's Pool Hall later that night, as Autumn Matthews was quietly escorted to a small, grimy cell, wondering which of her many enemies had finally caught up with her. Denying the charges would be pointless, she realized, as she shivered in her new home. After all, revenge *is* a dish best served cold.

Chapter 23

Always and Forever

Oli knew what he **wanted** to do, he just wasn't sure how to go about it. He wanted it to be so special and unique, Mya would never forget the moment.

Sterling had convinced him to take the leap, but now that they were home, he'd decided to wait until he could make it perfect. Dinner and a proposal was just too regular for his woman; she deserved something extra, something over the moon. Thing was, he didn't even want her to have the slightest inkling of what he was up to. Mya was bossy and a bit nosey, so keeping her in the dark wasn't gonna be easy. A private beach, with rich, black sand, sparkling under the setting Mediterranean sun was the image in his head and come hell or high water, **that** was where and how he would ask her to be his wife. He would settle for nothing less.

It took Oli about two weeks to set his plan in motion. It would be risky but if he played his cards right and Mya cooperated, they would be engaged and well on their way to a brand new life together. The ring, a 3.2 carat French-Set Halo in white gold, was tucked safely away in his office safe, along with the plane tickets. He'd have to make up a real good story, he hated lying to her but the ends would justify the means. Mya knew he was in negotiations to become the newest partner in the firm, so maybe he could use that as a way to get her to agree to this short-notice, impromptu trip.

Later that evening, while they sat watching "Black Panther" for the 5th time, he laid the ground work with fingers crossed and a silent prayer.

BUSINESS LEFT UNFINISHED

"Hey bae, I gotta ask you something…Ned, you know Ned Perkins, the senior partner at the firm…well, Ned has invited me on a business/pleasure trip to Hawaii next week and I was just wondering if you'd like to tag along? Seeing as how I'm tryna land that partner position, I don't think I should refuse, but he made it clear I could invite someone…all expenses paid of course." He had to keep his tone real casual; she was so perceptive, she'd notice if he was too excited or anxious.

"Hawaii huh? You knew you better ask me or yo ass wouldn't be going but it does sound like fun. When next week?" So far so good.

"We would leave Thursday evening and get back in late Sunday night. Ned wanted to make sure the trip didn't disrupt the office routine too much…" Oh he was good, real good.

THE BOSS LADY

"Shit! I was planning to catch up on some office work this weekend. I'm really behind and I've got a couple of deadlines coming soon...so bae..." He interrupted her with the perfect solution.

"Just bring some of your work with us. I'll be in a few meetings and while I'm working, you can be working too. You can relax by the pool or whatever and work as long as you like. We'll be there for at least two days. Shit, you can even work on the plane..." He held his breath.

"You're right bae, I could be working while you're in those meetings and hell, I've wanted to visit Hawaii again for a minute. I just gotta focus and make sure I don't let the beauty distract me."

"So...does that mean you'll tag along for the ride?" He couldn't believe it was this easy.

"Hell yeah! Oh shit! I'm sure I don't have anything suitable for Hawaii. Let me go check my closet!"

"Oh boy…" he sighed, as she planted a quick kiss on his lips then ran off to plan what she…no *he*, would be buying for this trip. He didn't care…in less than a week, she would be one step closer to becoming Mrs. Oliver Hamilton III.

———————————

"Where is Ned and the rest of the crew from the firm?" They were seated on the jet but Mya didn't see any of his colleagues; she knew them all.

"I just found out they left about 2 hours ago. There was some sort of mix up with the tickets. Brad and his wife are coming in on a flight that leaves in about an hour. Ned was pissed! He wanted everyone at the hotel at the same time…something about some plans he'd made for tonight."

He'd foreseen her asking this question and was prepared. He prayed she wouldn't be too heated about all this lying.

"I bet he was…shit, I'd be pissed too if all my people were arriving at different times. Shit's crazy as hell. Let's just pray they didn't mess up the hotel reservations as well. Then I'm gone be pissed right along with Ned…" They laughed, settling in for the almost ten hour flight from Cleveland to Maui. Just as planned, Mya had brought her work with her and there was no time like the present to get started. Preparing the small work space before her, she popped in her ear buds and went in.

Oli reclined, getting comfortable, with a smug grin on his face. He was proud of himself for pulling this off, thanking God that all was going well. She knew they were headed to Hawaii; she didn't know they were headed to a private beach in Maui. Ned **had** actually been a part of arranging that for him. **Waianapanapa State Park** was legendary for its beauty, history and its black sand beach. Ned had a business associate with ties to the Park, thus helping Oli get access to one of the secluded stretches of beach. It was perfect! He accredited it to Divine Intervention because there's no way *he* could have worked it out more perfectly. And, to top it off, this particular weekend, the Park was hosting some type of traditional event in honor one of the legendary volcanoes. There was one thing Oli knew for sure...the right amount of money could buy just about anything. Just about. They would have to keep a low profile and be mindful of the natives that still lived near the Park, but his plans didn't include them doing a lot of stuff other folk needed to see. He closed his eyes, picturing again in his mind the scene he'd replayed over and over...

"Aloha and welcome to our beautiful Maui..." Oli thought he was still dreaming until Mya elbowed him.

THE BOSS LADY

"Get up bae, we're here!" She was as excited as a little girl on her first trip out of town; her eyes were absolutely sparkling.

As passengers began to remove their seat belts to retrieve their bags from the overhead compartments, Mya squealed in delight. She hadn't been to Hawaii since her second year in college; best believe she was looking forward to this. She grabbed Oli's hand, making her way off the plane as soon as she could.

"Aloha nui loa..." the beautiful stewardess said, as she draped the customary Lei around their necks.

"Aloha nui loa..." they responded simultaneously. At the entrance to the hotel, the were draped again, before being escorted to their room. The **Travaasa Experiental Resort** in Hana was gorgeous, the balcony view breathtaking, the sights and smells tantalizing. There was a five hour time difference, so in Cleveland, it would have been 12:45 am; in Maui, it was 7:45 pm. They were both too excited to even notice the change.

Once their luggage arrived, they both stripped down, jumping in the shower together. As tempted as Oli was, he kept his hands to himself so they could dress and be out. He had plans that didn't include sex in a hotel room, no matter how lavish that room might be. In his briefcase was a map with directions on the fastest way to the black sand beach from the Hotel. They could actually see the Park lights from their balcony. Packing an overnight bag with all the essentials, grabbing their room key card and Mya's Louis tote, they headed for the path that led to their spot. The ring was secured on a chain, double pinned to the pocket of Oli's white t-shirt.

Mya, in a pale peach, cotton, off the shoulder Maxi dress, was all bronzed and stunning. Oli wore simple white Bermuda shorts, a white short-sleeved t-shirt with a pale peach short-sleeved button down over the tee. They both wore white leather sandals and looked like royalty, as they made their way through the Hotel lobby, out the huge double glass doors and around the side of the massive structure. The directions were simple and on point. Within minutes, they were entering the Park through what appeared to be a secret passage.

There was lush greenery and exotic flowers everywhere. Strange rock structures lined the secluded beach and the black sand gleamed in the last rays of the setting sun. Mya stopped, holding her hand over her mouth; the sight was nothing short of miraculous. It gave her a fresh sense of hope to know such unspoiled beauty still existed in the world. She'd had no idea where Oli was taking her but now, she never wanted to leave. They stood there, holding hands for what seemed like an eternity because time stood still in a place like this. It's uncanny how they both thought, *this is as close to God as it gets on earth*, in the same moment as the sun set on the water and it came to life. Every color in the rainbow and maybe a few that weren't, made an appearance on the water. So vivid and clear, it almost hurt the eyes to see. Oli tugged slightly on her hand, signaling it was time to keep moving.

After another five minutes of walking, they came to what appeared to be a clearing in the greenery and bam...the breathe caught in their throats. Sitting nestled among the flora was a small hut, surrounded by lanterns and lit torches. It boosted a thatch roof and was shaped like a wooden and straw gazebo. A stone walkway led to the small porch with two wicker rocking chairs. A stone brazier, lit and burning bright was off to one side, a man-made pond with a waterfall on the other. It was the simplicity of the structure, among all the lavish beauty of nature that made it so alluring. As Oli took a step to enter the hut, Mya restrained him, concern in her voice.

"Bae…what are you doing? I'm sure this is somebody's home. You can't just go…" He silenced her by placing a finger on her lips.

"Yes, it is somebody's home…it's **our** home away from home, at least for the next two days…"

Eric experienced a melt down worth writing home to mama about; all this shit with Mya and Autumn had really been stressing a nicca more than he'd realized. Don't get it twisted, he was overjoyed with how the plan had worked and feeling really good about finally nailing that lil thot, it was just that reverting back to many of his old ways and dealing with some of his old cronies had him feeling some type of way. He wasn't that person anymore, or, at least he thought he wasn't, but truth be told, the "snake" still in him had thoroughly enjoyed the whole process.

BUSINESS LEFT UNFINISHED

A few nights after the Feds raided Autumn's shop, Eric woke in a cold sweat, shaking something fierce. An unexplained fear gripped him and it took several hours for him to relax enough to go back to sleep. However, it continued to happen every night for the next week. It wasn't a nightmare, he didn't dream. It felt more like a warning and he was more than a little troubled. He remembered the crazy dreams, almost like premonitions, he'd had about Mya and Autumn, thinking to himself, *Oh shit, what's about to happen now*?!

When, after two weeks, the madness hadn't subsided, Eric decided he needed to go see his favorite therapist, Penelope Gee. He hadn't had a good night's sleep in close to two weeks, which was affecting his performance at work and had him looking like death. Dark circles were forming around his eyes, he was growing out a beard and he felt like shit.

He and Dr. Gee had once been lovers. He'd never been her patient but knew a few of her clients. She was good at what she did, in more ways than one, but theirs had been a purely sexual relationship. She was all about her money, her practice and her position. Now he figured he needed her professional skills just as much as he'd once needed her other skill set.

He called her office early one Tuesday afternoon, setting an appointment to see her, after hours, the following day. Yes, she saw clients after hours and they paid dearly for it. When she saw his name on her appointment calendar, she immediately called him.

"Hey Eric, how are you? Your name just popped up on my appointment schedule and I'm curious. Is this professional or something else?" She secretly hoped it was something else. Eric was the one that had got away, she not realizing how much she liked him until he was gone. Not being one to chase any man, when it appeared to be over between them, she'd walked away with pride, but she'd often wondered what if…

"Hey Penny…uhm…it's professional. How you been doing? I saw the article on your practice so I'm assuming you doing real good." Dr. Penelope Gee was the one person from Eric's new life he could keep it 100 with. They'd known one another for years, ever since their first year in college and she'd met "the snake" one or two times. Plus, Penny was from his side of the tracks, a hood rat determined to be, do and have more. He was extremely proud of her accomplishments and he let her know it.

Dr. Gee could hear the dullness in his voice, knowing something was wrong. "Okay E, what's going on with you? I can hear it in your voice. We go way back, so this one is on me…no charge."

THE BOSS LADY

Over the next three hours, Eric talked like he hadn't since the 8th grade, when he was trying to keep the school bully from whipping his ass. He shared everything, from his break up with Mya to the situation with Autumn, and even some stuff he hadn't known he needed to share.

Being a true professional, as well as a friend, she listened intently, dissecting his words and tone in hopes of getting to the root of the problem. She could instantly tell he was deeply troubled, steering him quickly toward a manic depressive episode. Few people knew about his bouts with depression, the circumstances of the last few weeks taking him back to that depressed state of mind and causing these night terrors. The things that led to depression and manic depressive behavior could be as small as a broken nail or as large as a tragedy.

It was obvious to her, he hadn't been guarding his thoughts and feelings well enough, allowing present and past issues to build up in his sub-conscious, producing the thoughts and emotions that facilitate a depressive state. In layman's terms, all this shit going on had him hella depressed, even though he didn't yet realize this. That's why *she* was the one with a PhD in Psychology.

Dr. Gee let it all pour out of him, it was the first step to getting him back on track; the necessary emptying of the mind and emotions. Eric had to admit he felt totally drained after their hours long talk, if you could call it that. He'd talked; she'd simply listened, only asking a provoking question here or there. Letting it all out was like a burden lifting from his muscled shoulders.

That night, he slept soundly for the first time in over two weeks, so Penelope was pleasantly surprised when he called the following evening. Having canceled their appointment, remember this one was on her, she hadn't expected to hear from him so soon. She'd explained to him what was happening and how to rectify it, so why was he calling?

Eric had slept for eleven plus hours straight, woke up totally exhausted and gone back to sleep for another four hours. When he woke the second time, he felt more like himself, although he was still tired as hell. His first thought, upon awakening, was of Penny; he wanted to see her. So, without giving it too much thought, he called and told her just that.

"Hello…" Dare she hope this call was that something else?

"Hey Penny, did I catch you at a bad time? I'd like to maybe meet up somewhere for a drink or something."

"Nope, my last patient just left and I'm starving…" The door was open, he would either walk through it or not.

Yes! "Good, cause so am I and I can't think of anyone I'd rather share a meal with right now…"

The diamond on her finger sparkled all the more against the blackness of the sand. The stars were working overtime to try to outshine this gorgeous work of art. They laid naked, on a thick blanket, on the beach; the only light was the stars, the moon, the fire in the brazier and the glow radiating from within them both. Mya couldn't believe how much her life had changed in the last two hours, let alone two months.

The proposal had been simple with few words. In this heaven on earth, words weren't really necessary. He'd taken her inside the hut, where the most precious white orchids waited, resting on a small ornate table in what was the sitting room. Champagne chilled in a silver bucket of ice, on a silver platter, with two of the most delicate champagne flutes she'd ever touched. A black, white and yellow homemade blanket was draped across the only chair in the room, so thick and plush, it felt like clouds must feel.

Without a word, Oli grabbed the blanket, the bucket and the wine glasses, handing those to her. She also took the orchids. Together they extinguished the lanterns and torches then headed for the beach. The sounds of water, night birds and nature surrounded them. In a spot just down the beach from the hut, they found a CD player, so it was there that they spread the blanket.

Oli hit the play button and the soft, low lyrics of Heatwaves "**Always and Forever**" filled the night air. It was Mya's favorite song of all time. Her mother had once played it constantly and Mya still loved it. It was in this instance, she realized he was up to something and there was no business trip with Ned. Yet, she kept quiet, waiting to see how this would play out.

BUSINESS LEFT UNFINISHED

Oli tapped his shirt pocket, making sure the ring was still there, got on his knees in front of her, brought forth that 3.2 in diamonds and simply said…

"Please make me the happiest man on earth by agreeing to share the rest of your life with me and to allowing me to love you, always and forever." It had been like a dream, it was so real, yet unreal.

Despite the intoxicating beauty of the moment and her surroundings, Mya took the time to reflect, calm her racing heart and make her decision based on truth and reality. They'd only met a few months prior, under dubious circumstances, yet deep within her, she knew she loved him, he loved her and this was right. But was it enough to build a marriage and a lifetime? *Yes*, came the response from that small, still voice inside. So, she responded to Oli in like manner.

"Yes." She said it with quiet confidence and assurance. It wouldn't always be easy or good but it **would** always and forever be right.

They made love there on the beach, consummating the union of their hearts and souls, lost in the beauty of each other and the black sand beach of Maui.

Chapter 24

<u>Meet Me At The Altar</u>

It was the wedding of the century as far as they were concerned. A small, intimate affair with only close friends, family and a few business associates. Mya was Angel's Maid of Honor, of course, with Felice and her new friend Deja as her only two bridesmaids. Sterling flew his cousin and best friend Paul out to be his Best Man. Derrick and Rashid, two more friends from his hometown Cleveland, were his groomsmen. Her niece Ariyah was her flower girl and she was simply adorable.

Angel's gown was simple, yet so truly classical and elegant. A fitted, sleeveless dress of silver satin that fishtailed at the bottom in the back and stopped just above the top of her silver satin slippers. White lace flowers were delicately embroidered throughout the dress, matching the 100 inch scarf of lace she wore as her veil, wrapped around her shoulders then cascading down her back on either side to become her train. It was exquisite in its simplicity and the fit clung to her every curve when she moved.

Mya's dress was red satin and made just like Angel's without the fishtailing in the back and the embroidered flowers; it just fell straight down to the tops of her red satin shoes. Her scarf was sheer red, 70 inches long, wrapped around her neck and shoulders from the front and cascaded down her back. It wasn't long enough to be a train, yet it flowed beautifully when she walked. The bridesmaid's dresses were silver satin with sleeves that stopped just below the elbow, they were off the shoulder, accompanied by red scarves with white pearl embellishments, draped around the neck and falling to the middle of the back. They wore silver shoes as well. Each woman's hair was pulled back into a low, dramatic bun.

BUSINESS LEFT UNFINISHED

Mya and the bridesmaids wore thin, silver hooped earring with rhinestones and no other jewelry. Angel wore ruby and silver tea-drop earrings to match Sterling's cuff-links. Mya wore red satin above the elbow gloves, Angel's white satin gloves stopped just under her armpits and the bridesmaids wore regular red satin gloves.

Sterling looked like a prince in a white, traditional 3-piece tux. His lapel was silver satin, as was the vest and lapel kerchief. His cuff-links were ruby and silver, finishing the ensemble with white velvet slippers. The other three men in the wedding party wore black 3-piece tuxedos, with red satin vest, lapel kerchief and black velvet slippers. Felice and Mya had been a little unsure about the splash of red color, but it had turned out fabulously. The contrast between the bride in all silver and white and Mya, in all red, was a huge success!

THE BOSS LADY

The church pews were decorated with white and red rose bouquets with deep silver ribbons. They alternated, white then red then white…all the way to the altar. On each side of the altar, sat a huge arrangement with red, white, and silver carnations. These same color carnations were used to create Angel's bridal bouquet. Even Sterling's pastor was dressed in wedding colors, with a red 3-piece suit, the vest and shoes in black. The tables in the reception hall were draped in white satin with red napkins stuffed in each wine glass, everything else was in silver.

It was a magical day, full of love, life and laughter. Oli, like always, took his queue from Sterling. He paid close attention to the small details, things like the gifts Sterling had bought for everyone in the wedding party, the fresh flowers used in everything, the simplicity yet elegance of the entire wedding. The music played at the reception and the horse-drawn carriage Sterling had hired to bring the ladies to the church, then to take the newly married couple from the church to the reception hall. Sterling had thought of everything, being in tune with himself and his bride, and it showed.

They danced and laughed into the wee hours of the morning. The bride and groom left the reception around 10 pm, heading to the airport to start their life as husband and wife in sunny Hawaii. That was Oli's wedding gift to them, an all expense paid honeymoon on the black sand beaches of Maui. Everyone else stayed, celebrating the life and love of the newly weds. The food was plentiful and delicious, the champagne flowed; the company and music was enjoyable, and life was good.

Sterling's cousin Paul had brought along his fiance, who was a videographer. She produced a wedding CD, along with a customized wedding photo album, capturing the joy and beauty of that special day. After the honeymoon, they watched it twice, then tucked it away to show their children in the future. A future that seemed so bright and promising on that awesome day. The CD and the photo album would one day become more priceless to Sterling than life itself.

Chapter 25

<u>Serve It Up</u>

Eric couldn't believe how good Mya looked, she was positively glowing! Marriage and pregnancy certainly agreed with her. Maybe it was time for him to go ahead and take the plunge.

About a week after he and Dr. Gee had rekindled their romance, at her request, he'd called Mya to settle all their unfinished business. She'd agreed to meet him for coffee and they'd had a nice chat. He still cared deeply for her, as she did for him, but they both realized it had never been real love.

"Damn, you look great! It's good to see you Mya. First, I want to apologize for that whole Autumn situation. I would never deliberately put you in harm's way."

THE BOSS LADY

Mya shook her head, waving off his apology. "There's nothing for you to apologize for...there was no way you could have known she was a nympho criminal. Bitch was just crazy and we know she was crazy long before she met you. It's good to see you too...you look happy."

"I am and so do you. What's been going on with you?" Mya proceeded to tell him all about Angel, her pending marriage and Oli. For just an instant, he experienced a twinge of jealousy, letting it have its moment then pushing it out of his mind. *That* had been almost two years ago.

Now they were seated across from each other in the cafe, as he interviewed her about her new book. Yes, Mya had finally finished her book and was in the middle of a promotion campaign that included newspaper, magazine and even one television interview. Eric had again won an award for one of his stories, but not the story he'd been working on when the Autumn scandal took place. The story that had propelled him into the assistant editor position had been on Autumn and the secret lives people live when they are involved in all types of criminal activity. He had went hard on that story, following Dr. Gee's advice to put it in print as part of his healing process. That woman just understood him in a way no one else did. She was the ying to his yang and he was grateful she'd come back into his life.

After the interview, the talked about life, relationships, marriage and the future. Mya urged Eric to ask Penny to marry him, he wasn't getting any younger and he didn't need to waste anymore time.

"Look, you love her and she loves you. Every time I see you, you look even happier than the time before and I know most of that is about Penelope. Stop bullshitting nicca and do the damn thing!" Still the same outspoken, bossy Mya, but if settling down made you as happy as she looked, he was all for it!

"Okay…okay! I'll do it! But, if I call you for some pointers, you better answer the phone…"

"I got you dude! I promise you won't regret it. I never thought I could be this happy and I sincerely want that for you Eric." She had convinced him. He and Dr. Gee were planning a weekend getaway, he would pop the question then.

––––––––––

Oli closed the file on his desk, stretched, then sat back in his chair. The case had been difficult, stressing him to the point of sleepless nights, but Ned had trusted him with it and he had won! It had been his first case since making partner, and the only case he'd worked on in the last almost two years. Ned refused to let him work on anything else. It was a billion dollar lawsuit, demanding all of his attention.

With the case won and closed, Oli could concentrate on other things, like the new house he intended to buy Mya. With the baby coming, they would need the space, plus, she deserved a new home for putting up with him the last nine months. She'd been patient and supportive throughout his transition in the firm and this helacious case. He had already put a deposit down on the house and was expecting to have everything finalized by the time Angel came to visit. It would all be a huge surprise for Mya.

He was so proud of her! The book was a great success and she was working her butt off with advertising and promoting. She had even talked Angel into writing a book about her experience with Lincoln, it was set to release in a couple of months and they were all excited about that. Life was great and he couldn't wait to start his journey as a father. If it was anything like being a husband, he knew he would thoroughly enjoy it.

He and Mya listened to the baby's heartbeat every night, while either talking or reading to the growing fetus. With each day, the anticipation grew, as well as his nervousness. Would he be a good father? Would he know what to do in every situation concerning this wonderful child? He was absolutely certain she would be a great mother; she already was.

THE BOSS LADY

Oli locked his office safe, closed his briefcase and headed out of his office. He had an appointment with the Realtor and then he was off to the jewelry store. He had some special gifts he wanted to present to his wife, the beautiful mother of his unborn child.

Angel was beaming. She and Sterling had just opened their second coffee shop, *Angel's Brew*. Their signature tag line was *"A Little Taste of Heaven"*. So many blessings had been poured on them in the last two years, it was unbelievable. The book Mya had convinced her to write was set to release in a couple of months and she was going to visit her sister and pregnant best friend in a couple of weeks. Felice had even opened a second daycare center on the other side of Cleveland. It was as if God had chosen them for His special favor.

Angel had miscarried eight months ago and it was the depression that had driven her to start writing, thus prompting Mya to encourage her to write her story. Not only had it been therapeutic, she'd found she enjoyed writing and was good at it. She was already well into her second book, a fictional love story, set in the 1950's. Doing the research for the book was just as enjoyable as the actual writing. With her Realty license under her belt and the coffee shops, she and Sterling were becoming well known in Wisconsin as *the* up and coming power couple. Sterling had been promoted to Head Sales Director in his company and their were whispers he could be up for a Vice President position.

Oli called about a week before her flight to Cleveland to confirm the purchase of the new house. He'd been in constant contact with her and Sterling throughout the process because he valued their advice and opinions. How those two men had hit it off was a sure sign God was a real part of the plan. He made her promise to come stay with them and not go traipsing off to a hotel. Sterling would be in Europe on business while she was visiting in Cleveland.

"Hey Sis, just letting you know I'm about to leave for the airport...give my god daughter a kiss for me and I'll see you guys soon." Angel left the message on her voice mail since she didn't answer. She'd called twice, figuring Mya must be someplace where she couldn't answer her phone. She left a similar message for her sister and Sterling. *Why the hell is no one answering their damn phones?!*

The flight would be a short one and she was glad; she couldn't wait to see everyone. She was especially looking forward to playing with Mya's baby bump.

Sterling called just as she was about to board the plane. "Can't talk now bae...about to board. I love you and I'll call as soon as we land..."

"Love you..." was all she heard as she put her phone on "airplane" mode.

BUSINESS LEFT UNFINISHED

Maybe it was premonition or a warning from God, but just as she took her seat, another passenger screamed as her companion hit the floor. Apparently, the man was having a seizure and was rushed off the plane. If that wasn't enough, during the 20 minute delay, another plane had to make an emergency landing due to a passenger having a heart attack, which delayed Angel's flight another 20 minutes. On any other day, she would have taken these incidents as a warning and jumped off that plane but she was so excited about the visit, she dismissed these events and thought no more of them.

The final warning came in the form of some strange phenomenon taking place in the sky. As she looked out the window, antsy for the plane to take off, she thought she saw a white bird heading for the plane. As this object got closer, she thought she was seeing things. Whatever it was, it definitely had wings, but instead of a beak, she swore she saw a face on this bird. It almost looked transparent. Of course, she didn't recognize the face and it disappeared almost as quickly as it had appeared but the one thing that stuck in her mind was, the face seemed sad and the eyes had tears in them.

Angel blinked twice and it was gone. Thirty minutes later, as the stewardess came on to instruct them on what they had to do next, she realized the object had actually been an angel.

"Every one please stay seated and stay calm. Make sure you are fastened in your seat and your oxygen mask is in place. The captain is preparing for a crash landing..."

Angel's last thought was of Sterling as she whispered, "I love you my darling..."

"The plane went down 45 minutes out from Cleveland and they are saying there were no survivors..." Sterling's voice was void of any emotion, tone, inflection, anything. He sounded dead. Mya couldn't believe what she was hearing. This had to be some type of sick joke or maybe, she was just dreaming and needed to wake the hell up, quick!

"...I'm headed out to the crash site and once I know more, I'll let you know…"

"Sterling, I…" she couldn't form a complete thought, less more a complete sentence.

"I know Mya…I know. Talk to you soon." And he was gone. Just as gone as Angel.

She couldn't believe it. She wouldn't believe it! There had to be another explanation. Angel couldn't be dead. She didn't feel like Angel was dead and she would know, wouldn't she? Angel was her dearest, closest friend…like a sister. Surely she would feel it in her heart if her friend was gone.

The news threw Mya into a state of shock, her body reacted and the next thing they knew, she was in labor. Oli rushed her to the hospital, scared out of his mind. She was only 23 weeks so this couldn't be good.

In the end, her doctors did everything they could to stop the birth but it was too late. The baby girl was stillborn at only 1lb, 14 ounces. Had she been born 3 weeks later, she probably would have made it. Oli was devastated; Mya, beyond despondent. He thought he might lose her too. She wouldn't talk, see any visitors, eat or even move. Even her doctors recommended she stay in the hospital, receiving psychiatric care. Her body would heal itself, it was her mind they were all concerned about.

Three weeks after the plane crash, Oli, Sterling, Felice, Eric and Dr. Gee laid baby Angel to rest beside the empty grave of her namesake, Angel Greenlee Larson. It had to be one of the saddest moments in all their lives. Dr. Gee was now working with Mya, making some head way but it was going to be some time before she was anywhere near normal.

BUSINESS LEFT UNFINISHED

Parked in a black sedan, on the other side of the cemetery, she watched the dismal scene before her. She didn't really give a damn about the others, her focus was Eric and the woman resting her head on his shoulder. She had no clue who this woman was but she was about to find out. It was the perfect place for a reunion… the cemetery. This way, they could just dig a hole and throw him and his bitch in it.

"Looks like they are about to leave. Show time!" She jumped out of the car, rushing toward the tiny grave site.

Eric couldn't believe his eyes! *What the hell is she doing here and how did she…*before he could finish his thought, she spoke.

"Hello Eric, how are you? Care to introduce me to your friend…" She was dressed in all black, as were the other mourners, except for her red leather gloves and the gleaming silver Glock she now pointed at him. Penelope recognized her immediately and the hood girl in her rose to the challenge.

THE BOSS LADY

"What the hell do you want? Can't you see we're in mourning and don't have time for your bull…" She fired the gun and Penny went down. It was just a flesh wound to the leg but it hurt like hell. Eric started towards her, but she leveled the gun at Penny's head.

"I wouldn't do that if I was you. I'll blow her brains all over this cemetery. You and I have some business we left unfinished that needs to be settled today. Once that's done, I will gladly put a bullet in you both and you can die together just as you thought you would live together…"

Autumn's voice sent a chill through them all but what was more horrifying were her eyes. They appeared to be completely black and the one tear clinging to her lashes, looked almost like blood. The wind blew furiously, an icy blast whistling threw the bare trees surrounding the cemetery. After all, revenge *is* a dish best served cold.

About The Author

Andrea Ellis, born and raised in Cleveland Ohio, now resides in Cincinnati Ohio. She is the proud mother of 2 daughters, has been married for 20 years and works for the University of Cincinnati Physicans.

Andrea always liked writing and English was her favorite subject in school. She first picked up a pen to write creatively as a teenager and has continued, off and on, throughout her life. She wrote her first novel in 2015 and it has taken 3 years to see it come to life in print.

Andrea has no idea where her future writing will take her, but she is definitely ready for the journey, wherever it may lead.

THE BOSS LADY

Author Andrea Ellis aka The Boss Lady

Made in the USA
Middletown, DE
08 February 2020